A LONELY NOTE

Kevin Stevens

A LONELY NOTE

Little Island

A LONELY NOTE

First published in 2015 by
Little Island Books
7 Kenilworth Park
Dublin 6W, Ireland

ISBN: 978-1-910411-31-5

A British Library Cataloguing in Publication record
for this book is available from the British Library

Cover designed by Pony and Trap
Insides designed and typeset by Oldtown
Printed in Poland by Drukarnia Skleniarz

Little Island receives financial assistance from
the Arts Council/An Chomhairle Ealaíon
and the Arts Council of Northern Ireland

10 9 8 7 6 5 4 3 2 1

For Michael Tallon

Acknowledgements

Siobhán Parkinson and Jason Sommer read multiple drafts of this novel and, as they always do, guided me with wisdom, tact and sure judgement. Gráinne Clear and Matthew Parkinson-Bennett brought their considerable editorial expertise to the book's production. My deep thanks to them all and to my wife, Janice, for her constant support.

Chapter 1

'HEY, FREAK – still on hunger strike?'

The question came from a cluster of kids at the entrance to the lunchroom. Though it wasn't really a question. Nasty laughter followed. Muttering. Tariq kept his head down. He walked up the foyer steps, past the trophy case, and underneath the flags of nation, state and school. He moved through the double doors beside the vice-principal's office. When they closed behind him it was like coming up for air after a long dive.

He got his clarinet case from his locker and went to the empty band room. He took a seat near the back and assembled his instrument. Pieced the joints and the bell together, carefully fitted the mouthpiece, moistened the reed and clamped it in place. He set up his music stand and played some scales. The routines soothed him, but the ugly nickname rang in his ears.

He had recognised the voice. Brad Jorgensen. A muscular kid in faded jeans and a torn sweatshirt who lived on the west side. He had a tattoo of a lightning bolt on his neck. Gold earring, heavy stubble, a sneer on his full lips. In gym class on the first day back at school, two weeks ago, Mr Thiel had asked Tariq how to pronounce his name. Someone at the rear of the roll call ranks cried out, 'Rhymes with *freak*.' Since then Brad had whispered the word in passing, shouted it in the street. He seemed to enjoy its sound. Already it had stuck. And other names. Twice on his way home Tariq had been harassed by Brad's friends, who threw rocks at him from the vacant lot beside the Dairy Queen and called him 'raghead' and 'camel jockey'.

After he had warmed up, Tariq practised the opening of *Rhapsody in Blue*. The band teacher, Mr Broquist, had scheduled the piece for the Thanksgiving concert, and Tariq had worked on the opening for ten days. But he couldn't get the *glissando* right. Instead of rising in celebration, it came out as one long, lonely note.

During Ramadan, Tariq was allowed to spend lunchtime in the band room. The principal had offered an empty classroom for prayer, but he and Yusef, the only other Muslim in the school, preferred to practise or study. Yusef was a senior who took advanced placement courses in physics and chemistry and had been accepted to the University of Chicago. He rarely spoke to Tariq, perhaps because his parents were Shias from Bahrain. His father was in the Muslim Brotherhood and his mother wore a burqa. He bristled when teachers assumed that he and Tariq were friends.

The door opened and Tariq went stiff with fear. But it was Rachel.

'Hey,' she said. 'This a private party?'

'You're not supposed to be here.'

'So sue me.'

She walked in and sat down. Dressed as usual in black leggings and a denim skirt and a man's striped shirt with the sleeves rolled up. Lots of plastic jewellery and curly dark hair spilling over her oversized glasses.

'Don't let me cramp your style,' she said.

He rested the clarinet crosswise on its case. 'It's no use. I'll never get it right.'

'Gershwin?'

'Yeah.'

'It's because he's Jewish. You're culturally disadvantaged.'

'Ha ha.'

Rachel was in most of his classes. She was a whiz at math but loved words. She was in the honours English programme, edited the school paper and wrote poetry. She also studied Hebrew on Wednesday afternoons at Temple Beth El.

He looked away. This always happened: she sought him out, joked with him, flirted. He could tell. He *knew*. And then he would clam up.

'Play that tune for me,' she finally said.

'We have history.'

'Not for ten minutes. Go on. Play.'

The only time he thought he could really open up to her was when he played *choubi*. She listened to bands like Vampire Weekend and Arcade Fire, but something about Iraqi folk music made her eyes go sexy.

He played 'Oh Girl, Stand Up', which his uncle had transcribed for him. Rachel loved the title and the music. And he loved that she loved it. The wild melody and the buzz of the reed against his lip made the clarinet feel like something alive in his hands. After a few seconds she stood up and danced in front of him, throwing her hair back, shaking her hips like a belly dancer, lifting and waving her arms so that her orange and yellow bracelets slid nearly to her elbows. Embarrassed to look at her body, he focused on her feet, clad in black ballet flats with small gold bows. They glided across the polished wooden floor in time with the rhythm.

'God, those notes,' she said when he was finished. 'Where do they *come* from?'

The music was familiar to him. He had heard it all his life. It was her dancing that made it exotic. That made him feel like a snake charmer.

'So how come I can't do the *Rhapsody* gliss?'

'You'll get it. Don't worry.'

A picture formed in his mind. A picture that often came to him. In it, Rachel lay beside him in bed, gazing at him with the same hooded look she had when she listened to him play. One of her hands lay on his bare chest.

He opened the instrument case and began to disassemble the clarinet.

'Are you OK?' she said.

'I'm fine.'

She watched him place the pieces in their felt-lined pockets. His hands shook. Not so much, but enough so she could tell.

'Is it that asshole Brad?'

He said nothing. She took her glasses off and wiped the lenses with the hem of her shirt. The excitement of her dance had faded. But she was still smiling.

The class bell cut across his silence. From the hallways came sounds of yelling, laughter, locker doors banging.

'Back to the grind,' she said at last. 'History class. Are you coming?'

'You go ahead.'

She lingered, shrugged and left.

AFTER school, he went to the resource centre. If he waited long enough before walking home, he would avoid Brad and his friends.

He passed the time watching YouTube videos of Iraqi pop music. No clarinets, but ouds and flutes and drums, usually accompanying male singers with oily hair and white suits with wide lapels. And women dancing. Always dancers. They wore heavy eye make-up and tight, frilly dresses and chunky jewellery.

When they moved they thrust out their breasts and hips, shaking their bodies and smiling at the camera while the zanboor drum rattled like a machine gun.

He felt himself going hard and shut down the computer. When Rachel danced, his whole body responded, not just his dick. But he enjoyed looking at the dancers and thinking of her.

Dizzy with hunger, he wondered what his mother would make for the evening meal. Sunset was another four hours away. Before lunch hour he'd eaten a chocolate bar he had bought on the way to school and hidden in his locker. Ate it so quickly and furtively he'd hardly tasted it. Afterwards he felt unclean and even hungrier.

At four o'clock he left the school by the rear entrance, passing the computer lab and civics room. Both were empty. Above the entrance to the civics room hung a satin banner that read: WE ARE DEFINED BY HOW WE TREAT THOSE DIFFERENT FROM OURSELVES. Below the sign, Mr Kholandi polished the hallway floor. He was from Syria. He was much shorter than Tariq and wore a moustache that looked like a wire brush. He struggled so much with the big polisher that he didn't hear Tariq say hello.

The day was bright and hot, as hot as it had been all summer, and the rustling cottonwoods cast checkerwork shadows on the walkway. He hiked his schoolbag up his shoulder and switched the clarinet case from one hand to the other and headed across the parking lot, through the buzz of crickets and a breeze tinted with the smell of alfalfa.

He didn't notice the boys until he was out from under the trees. Four of them, including Jorgensen, sat on the hood of a car eating hamburgers. The sun was behind them so he couldn't see their faces.

As he angled away from them, heart jumping, they slid off the car, ran across the parking lot, and encircled him.

'It's the freak,' Brad said. 'Where are you going?'

Tariq did not answer. He set his clarinet case on the ground.

'Running home to say your prayers?'

'No.'

'I thought all you people did was pray. When you're not blowing yourself up.'

The football team was on the practice field beyond the parking lot. Whistles, shouts, the clash of shoulder pads. Through the chain-link mesh of the fence, Tariq could see the coaches in their gold polo shirts and maroon shorts.

'I'd be praying if I was you,' another boy said. 'Praying you don't get your ass kicked.'

The rest of them laughed. Hard laughter. One of them was still eating a burger, and the smell of it made Tariq's stomach turn. He thought about running back to the school and getting Mr Kholandi, but what would he say? Some boys are being mean to me?

Before summer vacation, Mrs Gunderson, who taught history and civics, had invited Imam Mohammad from Tariq's mosque to speak at assembly. Tariq and Yusef had been forced to sit beside the imam on the dais while he spoke, on and on, about the Five Pillars of Islam. Before that day, nobody had ever bothered Tariq about his religion.

'Those faggots in the Middle East, I saw them on TV,' Brad said. 'Bending over with their shoes off and facing the same direction like a bunch of robots. Wearing those fucking beanies and praying to Allah for the takeover of America.'

'Destruction of America.'

'That right, freak?' Brad said. 'When you bend over, do you pray for planes to hit the White House?'

'No.'

'Bend over now,' the kid with the burger said.

When Tariq did not move, the kid kicked his clarinet case so that it tumbled across the tarmac. He thrust a dirty food wrapper into Tariq's face. The smell made him want to vomit, and he pushed the paper away. Brad grabbed the shoulder bag, threw it to the side, and wrestled Tariq to the ground, pinning him down. Tariq struggled and kicked, but Brad was strong. The other boys sat on his legs and took off his shoes.

'Woo-hoo,' they cried, laughing and throwing the shoes into the bushes.

'See you pray now, dickhead.'

He knew what they were going to do before they did.

Two of the boys pinned his legs while the other unbuckled Tariq's belt and unbuttoned his pants. He struggled and squirmed and cursed.

'Haiwan, beljuhanem!'

The Arabic curse surprised him – he had meant to speak in English. The strange sounds enraged the boys even more. They whisked off his pants. Tariq kicked as hard as he could and struck one of them in the leg.

'You asshole,' the boy shouted. He grabbed the waistband of Tariq's boxers. He hesitated, and Tariq prayed, prayed in the most precise Arabic, that he be spared the ultimate shame. But the boy ripped the boxers off him, exposing to the bright sunlight Tariq's penis, white and shrivelled in its nest of hair.

Time slowed, sound stopped, the sun hung high in the sky. The bullies stared, mouths open, as if shocked themselves by what they'd done. When Brad let go of him, Tariq curled up, grabbed his pants, and pulled them on. Without meaning to, he sobbed.

Brad barked a laugh and drifted away. The others followed.

Slowly, Tariq stood up. His bag had opened and his notes and pens and books were scattered on the ground. The clarinet case was scuffed and scraped. His torn boxers lay on the tarmac like a broken flower. Beyond the fence a whistle shrieked, a football was punted high in the air, the players shouted. He wiped his nose and, reaching for his bag, saw two girls hugging their schoolbooks to their chests and staring at him from a window on the third floor.

Chapter 2

HIS MOTHER called him twice for *iftar*. When he did not leave his bedroom, his father came upstairs and entered without knocking.

'Tariq, your mother has put the food on the table.'

'I'm not hungry.'

He was lying on his bed, facing the wall, his hands clasped between his knees. His shoulders ached and his legs throbbed where they had been cut and scratched.

'Son. Turn around.'

After a moment he rolled over and looked up at his father. He was dressed in his hospital clothes: blue cotton suit, white shirt, dark blue tie. In his jacket pocket was a protective plastic pouch holding several pens and a small chrome flashlight.

'Of course you are hungry,' he said. 'It has been more than twelve hours. But you don't sense it. Your hunger is hidden, like an animal in the trees.'

When his father used these old expressions, his tone changed. Tariq called it his master's voice. As if he were teaching a lesson.

As if hunger had anything to do with it.

'We are in the month of patience, Tariq. He who fasts will have his sins forgiven and will be delivered from the fire.'

'Yes, Baba, I know.'

Tariq thought of the Snickers bar he had gobbled in high daylight, the crunch of the peanuts and the sticky caramel he had barely tasted. And though he had washed his face and hands and changed his clothes as soon as he got home, he could still smell the sickening food wrapper the bully had thrust in his face.

'Get up,' his father said.

Tariq stood. He was dizzy. 'I'm just not hungry,' he said. 'It has nothing to do with the fast.'

'Fasting is one of the Pillars of Islam. I don't have to tell you that.'

'No. You don't.'

'Like your prayers. Have you performed *maghrib?*'

'Yes,' Tariq lied.

His father looked at the rumpled bedspread and said in a low voice, '*Fast* is not the best way to put it. In the ancient Arabic the word means "abstain". Not just food. We abstain from false talk and impure deeds.'

'I know all this. I'm not *hungry*.'

Tariq stared at the floor. His body burned with shame, and his eyes were hot with tears.

'Let's eat, son.'

His father patted him on the shoulder and smiled, as if he knew everything.

FOR the evening meal his mother served dates and sweetened milk, followed by tabouleh and hummus and fried eggplant. Stewed lamb with yogurt. Sweet and savoury breads and sliced vegetables. The dishes covered the table, and Tariq could not avoid seeing and smelling the food. He nibbled this and that. It was all like sawdust in his mouth.

At college his mother wore traditional clothes, though she was always stylish. Her head scarves were bright and pleated, her cloaks made of silk or chiffon and delicately embroidered.

During Ramadan she also wore her scarf at home, which made her face look rounder, her eyebrows darker.

'Is that a new hijab?' his father often asked. He didn't like the loud colours and fancy patterns. He believed a woman's dress should be not just modest but severe.

She would tilt her head, pat the silk with the tips of her fingers and smile at Tariq. 'I don't recall the Qur'an saying anything about what colours I should wear.'

'It has nothing to do with the Qur'an.'

'So what has it to do with?'

'Tradition.'

His mother laughed. A musical laugh, like the tinkling of a triangle. 'Well, *my* tradition allows for pastels.'

But his father said nothing about the hijab this evening. She peered at Tariq and spooned baba ganoush onto his plate. 'Eat, *habibi*, eat. Don't make me feel as if I did all this cooking for nothing.'

'Leave the boy alone, Zaida,' his father said. 'He'll eat.'

Zaida taught chemistry at the state university. During Ramadan, the administration permitted her a lighter schedule so she could come home early and prepare *iftar*. She cooked for the family table and for the mosque, where they ate two, sometimes three evenings a week.

His father ate slowly, frequently wiping the corners of his mouth. His beard, though streaked with grey, was carefully trimmed and combed. His eyes were deep-socketed, long-lashed and intensely dark. At dinner his movements were over-refined, as if to emphasise that a long day of hunger would not reduce him to vulgar expressions of greed or haste.

'I met with the committee today,' he said. 'You'll be interested in this, Tariq. The Az-Zahra Madressah has challenged our congregation to a football match.'

'You mean soccer?'

'It's football, Tariq. That is what I choose to call it.'

He meant soccer.

Zaida's large eyes moved from husband to son and back. 'That's not a bad idea, Malik,' she said. 'Something to bring the communities closer.'

At Monroe General, Tariq's father was known as Mal. In his house and at mosque he was always Malik.

He snorted and waved a piece of bread at her. 'You want to be closer to those Africans?'

Most of the students at the madressah were recently arrived Shias from Uganda and Nigeria. They did not have their own mosque, but met in a basement below a furniture store in Monroe. Their imam was Iranian.

'Fasting brings true sympathy for the poor and needy,' she said.

Malik scowled. 'You think that ayatollah is poor?'

'Hamid is no ayatollah. And he is a decent man. I had lunch with his wife last week, and she told me they have secured funding for a new mosque.'

'Funding from where is what I want to know.'

'It doesn't matter where. They deserve a proper place of worship as much as we do. As anyone. When will you play? Soon?'

'The match? After Ramadan. *If* we agree to it. You can play for us, Tariq.'

'I don't play soccer any more.'

'You won't have a choice.'

Zaida examined him again. 'Tariq, are you all right?' She touched his chin and nudged his face up. 'You're white as milk. What's the matter? Malik, look at him.'

His father kept eating. 'He's weak. From fasting. He'll be fine after some lamb.'

His father did not like being consulted outside the hospital. 'I'm a doctor all day,' he often said. 'At home I am just another citizen.'

'He looks awful, Malik.'

'I'm sick,' Tariq said. 'I told Baba.'

'You told me no such thing. You said you weren't hungry.'

His mother led him away from the table. While he undressed and got into bed she soaked a towel in cold water.

'I don't need that,' he said when she tried to lay the wet cloth on his forehead.

He turned towards the wall.

'It will help you feel better.'

'No it *won't*.'

She went to the door and lingered. He could feel her gaze on his back for several moments. She shut the door and returned downstairs.

AS dusk turned to darkness, Tariq lay awake in his bed, watching the headlights of passing cars stripe the ceiling and listening to the murmur of his parents in the kitchen. At nine o'clock his father turned on the television news and his mother slipped into Tariq's bedroom without switching on the light. Later he would find a slice of lemon cake and a glass of sparkling water on his dresser.

After an hour he heard them go to bed. He let another hour pass, and drank the water. He used the bathroom and washed his face and hands and brushed his teeth, avoiding his image in the mirror.

He did not return to bed. This part of the night was the worst, when the house was dark and still and he couldn't sleep. It was the time when he thought of Rachel and tried hard to keep himself pure – though more often than not he ended up masturbating. He couldn't help himself, even though he knew how guilty and depressed he would feel afterwards.

But tonight the darkness was filled with the humiliation of the parking lot. Somehow, the picture that filled his mind was from above, as if a different part of himself had hovered over the incident, like a hummingbird. He lay pinned to the ground, his pale limbs and circumcised dick there for the wide world to see. He shuddered and closed his eyes, but the image only brightened. And tomorrow, the whole school would know: Brad and his friends would brag about it, and even if they were too scared to say anything in case they got into trouble, the girls on the third floor would tell their friends.

Outside his window, the wind moved through the treetops. A line of poplars screened the Mussams from their neighbours, an old couple named Greenbriar who rarely left their house. The street was a quiet one, with hardly any young people. An ordinary American street, with oak trees shading the cracked sidewalks, the stars and stripes hanging above limestone porches and lawns that were well trimmed and too green to be true.

On the outside, the Mussam house looked like its neighbours: two-storied, with wooden shingles and sash windows and steep dormers. It even had a wall-mounted mailbox and a doormat monogrammed with *M*. But his parents kept the inside like an Iraqi home – pink walls, embroidered nomadic rugs on polished hardwood, net curtains and fancy pillows and brass trays. A lacquered jewellery box painted with scenes from *Gilgamesh*. Even his mother's plants felt different from those in the homes of Tariq's friends. This difference disturbed him, as if he and his parents were pretending they were something they were not. Though it also made him miss Iraq.

But how could he miss a place that he had left when he was four years old? A place where the house he was born in was a pile of rubble? Where people were still being killed every week? Where, in his old neighbourhood of al-Jadriya, his uncle had been tortured by police from the Interior Ministry?

Yet in the silky warmth of the September night he easily recalled sensations from thirteen years ago. Sitting with his mother on the balcony, watching coloured lights play on the surface of the Tigris. The lonely call of the muezzin from Kadhimain Shrine at dawn. The smell of eggs and almonds when his auntie baked. The sudden rattle of gunfire and the way his father moved from the window with a look on his face as if he were in pain.

He switched on the gooseneck lamp at his desk and drew a notebook from its secret place at the rear of the bottom drawer. A gift from his uncle, it had red leather binding, black elastic flap-bands and smooth, unlined paper. On the cover, his name was embossed in gold in Arabic script. In this notebook Tariq wrote his poems in careful calligraphy, using a fountain pen he had bought in the university bookstore. Only final versions of poems were entered, usually after he had worked through many drafts with paper and pencil.

He reread his most recent entry, a poem without a title that he had written late in the summer:

> the river runs past my door
> in the rolling currents I see my death
> it stares at me like a shining fish
> telling me to come, come
> here to the cool water where all is peace

Once, before he had added this poem, he showed the notebook to Rachel. She read silently for a while, and when she finished she touched his arm and smiled and shook her head.

'What?' he said.

'I was going to say that you should send some of these to the school paper. But I don't think so.'

'Why?'

'They're too good.'

'I would say they're too personal.'

'Well,' she said. 'That too.'

He was tempted to tear out the new poem and rip it to pieces. But he closed the leather covers and set the notebook back in its place and switched off the lamp. For a long time he sat at the desk, staring into a dark so dense he could not see his own hand. Outside, a whip-poor-will called in the gloom.

Chapter 3

THE NEXT MORNING, a Friday, Tariq stayed in bed. Before dawn, he had heard his parents arguing as they ate their morning meal. He didn't have to hear their words to know what was being said. His father would doubt he was sick and want him to go to school and then to mosque. His mother would insist he not be disturbed.

After they left for work he went downstairs. His mother had left out rice porridge and stewed figs, and he found that he was hungry. Because he was ill, he was allowed to break the fast. He heated a large portion of porridge, added the fruit and made himself a cup of tea. He ate while watching *The Today Show*.

He would have to pretend to be sick for the whole weekend or have no choice but to return to school on Monday. Though in the sun-filled stillness of the empty house, Monday seemed a long way away.

He had a shower and put antiseptic cream on the cuts on his legs. He dressed in sweat pants and sweatshirt and tidied his room. His laptop and cell phone lay on the dresser. Both had been powered off since he got home from school yesterday. He ignored them. He imagined that the house was a big wooden ship, adrift in a borderless ocean. If he could only imagine time cut loose from the world as well. Though music would disguise the sense of the hours passing. It always did.

He laid out his clarinet but before practising spent an hour cleaning and fixing the case. It had done its job – the instrument was unscathed – but two of the corner hinges had been bent and the surface was heavily scarred. He removed, straightened and reattached the hinges and sanded and polished the leather. While he worked, he listened to the classical station his mother favoured. Rachmaninov's Piano Concerto No. 3, with its big chords and furious climaxes. The music echoed in the quiet house like the peal of church bells.

He turned off the radio after the first movement and played scales until he was warmed up. He forgot about the Gershwin and played a piece he knew well, the *vivace* of Brahms's first clarinet sonata. He played it straight through, without a single mistake, and when he finished he heard birds chirping in the poplars, as if in response. At that moment his body had that music buzz, that charged, floating feeling, as if he were a bird himself, not singing in the trees but high in the sky, motionless, wings tensed, riding a current of wind.

Then, like a firecracker exploding, the phone rang.

He waited several rings before answering. It was his mother.

'How are you, *habibi*?'

'OK.'

'You took so long to come to the phone.'

'I was in bed, Ommi. I'm sick, remember?'

'You ate.'

He hesitated, but admitted he had eaten.

'So you're feeling better.'

His mother's tone was careful but firm. Making statements, not asking questions.

'No,' he said. 'I have a headache. I couldn't sleep last night.'

'Well, if you are holding down your food, that's a good thing. I'll come home and fix you some lunch.'

'No.' His voice was sharper than he'd meant. 'I need to sleep. I'll wait until *iftar*. See how I feel.'

'Your father said he would bring some medicine.'

'He doesn't even think I'm sick.'

'Don't be disrespectful. Get your rest and wait for Baba.'

A long pause.

'Tariq?'

'Yes, Ommi.'

'Is everything all right?'

'I *told* you. I'm not feeling well.'

He wandered around the house, restless and anxious. It was another hot day, and the hiss of sprinklers and lazy sway of the crickets pulsed through the open windows. He fetched his binoculars from the closet and his book on the birds of Wisconsin. He scanned the back yard, still dense with summer green. Lilac bushes, hollyhocks, the old elm tree where the orioles nested. The back fence bound in Virginia creeper. Then the break in the line of spruce trees that allowed a long view through the empty fields behind the Greenbriars' house. In the past, this gap of sky had given him glimpses worth noting: during the summer he had spotted a pair of cedar waxwings and reported the sighting to the Audubon Society. But nothing today except a void of low cloud and heavy branches of evergreen, and when he put down his binoculars he felt uneasy, as if he were watched, not watching, and he closed the window and pulled the blind.

He retreated to the living room and turned on the radio, tuning to a college station that played world music, Indian and African and Arabic tunes with cool rhythms and trancelike melodies that he missed when playing Western music. Sometimes the station played Iraqi songs, but today it was kora music from Senegal. He lay on the divan and closed his eyes and let the sound wash over him.

Something in the West African rhythms called forth prayers and directions. The chant of the muezzin. The preaching of the imam.

Allahu Akbar. Ashada an La illah illa Allah ...

It was nearly one o'clock. His father would be at *jumu'ah*, performing Friday *salat*. This was the first Friday meeting Tariq had missed since last school year. *Each Friday, the angels take their stand at every gate of every mosque and write the names of the people as they appear.* These words, and so many others, he remembered from his early schooling. Along with the prayers, they tolled in his memory like musical phrases.

He could disbelieve, but he could not forget. Fasting was a pillar of Islam. It had special status because it was private, performed solely within the sight of Allah and more pleasing to him for its purity of intention. So Tariq had offended twice: by eating, and then by pretending he was sick. And all the worse for being within the sight of Allah alone.

If he were a believer, he had offended. But he did not believe.

The phone rang again. If only his parents would leave him alone.

'Hello.'

'Oh my God, are you not answering your *phone?*'

It was Rachel.

'I just did.'

'Your *cell.*'

'I'm out of credit. And it's off anyway. I'm sick.'

With Rachel's voice so suddenly and unexpectedly in his ear, it was as if he really *were* sick. His stomach churned. His breathing thickened. Because it was her, *there*, on the phone. But also because of what she might tell him about school that day.

'What's wrong?' she said.

'Just sick, really. Something I ate, I guess.'

'So much for fasting.'

'Whatever.'

'Aren't you online? I left you a comment on Facebook.'

'I'm sorry. Like I said. My phone's been off. And my laptop.'

There was a pause. He could hear her breathing. He wanted to know and he didn't want to know.

'So what did I miss?' he said.

'Miss?'

'In school today.'

'Oh, the usual bullshit. Mr Allen cried in class.'

'He *cried?*'

'Well, nearly. You know how we're doing the civil rights movement? He played a recording of Martin Luther King's "I Have a Dream" speech, and I swear to God I thought he was going to start blubbing any second. Like we all haven't heard that speech a million times.'

'At least he enjoys teaching. He's sincere.'

'He's sincere all right. Listen, I have some news.'

Tariq shifted the receiver from one ear to the other. 'Yeah?'

'I've signed up for dancing classes. At the college. The extension programme.'

'What, like ballet?'

'Middle Eastern dance.'

'Oh.'

'So when you play that tune, I'll really know how to move. I have to buy finger cymbals. And wear suitable attire. What do you think that means?'

'Loose clothes, I guess.'

'Not, like, *modest?*'

'I don't know. I really don't.'

There was an uneasy silence.

'Are you all right?' she said.

Before he could answer, she asked, 'Did anything happen yesterday?'

'What do you mean?'

'In school. Did anything happen?'

'Why?'

'I don't know. I heard some stuff.'

'What stuff?'

There was a fumbling sound, as if she had dropped the phone.

'Hey,' she said, 'can you meet me tomorrow? At Starbucks? I want to ask you about this dance thing and I have your homework from English.'

'What *stuff*, Rachel?'

More muffled sounds, and voices. Someone was speaking to her. She said to Tariq, 'I have to go. See you tomorrow. Two o'clock. The Starbucks beside the college bookstore.'

She hung up. Somewhere on the street a lawnmower started up. The sound of its motor scraped his nerves. He took a deep breath and carefully laid the receiver in its cradle.

She had heard something. And wouldn't tell him what. He could go on to Facebook and see if anyone had said anything. But who knew what he might find? He'd had the discipline to stay offline for twenty-four hours; there was no point in looking now. Rachel would tell him tomorrow. It would be better to hear it from her. Whatever it was.

But his insides were in turmoil and the heat of the house was suffocating. He stood in the middle of the living room, breathing deeply. The radio was still on, and under the drone of the lawnmower he became aware of its music. He turned up the volume. A saxophone, tenor by its pitch, with a piano playing chords behind it. Jazz, which they sometimes played on this station. But this music was unlike any jazz he'd ever heard.

The sax was crashing through rapid arpeggios, cascades of notes that ripped and looped into tangled clumps that were anguished and intense. Yet the notes were controlled. They were *meant*. Like the cry of a wild animal, but articulate and emotional and technically incredible. How was he doing it? How was the player getting those *sounds*?

He turned it up even louder. In spite of its violence, the music was soothing. It was as if the song was playing his own fears. He stood motionless amid the fancy pillows and antique rugs of the living room, listening the tune through to its drawn-out ending, hearing in its wrenching solo all the twisted feelings that had knotted him up since the day before. But feeling less anxious, too. As if the player were saying with his instrument: *Yes, I know, I do. I know what it's like.*

When the song was over, the radio host recited the details: 'Impressions', by John Coltrane. The announcer spoke his name reverently, as if he were a religious figure. As another jazz tune played, Tariq went into the kitchen and took a slip of paper from his mother's shopping pad and wrote down the name of the song while it was fresh in his mind. As he was writing, the radio went silent, and he heard his father call his name.

He went to the door of the kitchen. His father stood beside the radio. He was dressed in the loose gown and skullcap he wore to Friday prayers.

'Tariq. What are you doing?'

The cap made his father's head smaller and his bearded face darker and more severe. He held prayer beads in his right hand. Shiny circles stared up from the lower half of his gown, worn patches where his knees rubbed the fabric during prayer.

'The radio was on. It was blaring.'

'I was listening, Baba.'

His father looked him up and down, the grey sweat pants and college sweatshirt. Outside, the lawnmower choked to a halt.

'Why aren't you in bed?'

'I'm feeling a bit better. I'm sorry about the radio.'

'What was that you were listening to?'

'Jazz.'

'*Jazz*? On a Friday?'

'I was bored.'

His father flailed an arm towards the stairway. 'Go upstairs and get dressed.'

'I am dressed.'

'Proper clothes. We're going to mosque.'

His father was more aggressive when he wore his traditional clothing. And his body language changed: his limbs were looser, his gestures wilder. It had been over a year since he had hit Tariq, but when he did it was always while wearing a *dishdasha*. Though he had never hit him in front of Zaida.

'I can't go,' Tariq said. 'I'm sick.'

His father drew a package from the pocket of his gown. 'Do you know what this is? Your medicine. Your mother insisted I write a prescription. So now I have wasted seventeen dollars on top of everything else.'

He threw the package at Tariq's feet.

'Pick it up,' his father said.

When he bent down, his father raised an arm as if to hit him. Tariq flinched.

'You are a pig,' his father said in Arabic. Then in English: 'Do what you are told and get yourself ready for prayer.'

Tariq went to his room and slid the medicine from its paper bag and placed it on his dresser. He sat on the side of his bed and stared at his laptop, his phone, the locked bottom drawer of his desk.

His poster of the Berlin Philharmonic. The certificates of musical accomplishment and a photograph of his grandparents, whom he had never met, standing in front of the Baghdad Archaeological Museum in 1977.

Downstairs his father moved from room to room, closing windows with a bang.

Chapter 4

HAWTHORNE ROW was a busy street near the college lined with bookstores, restaurants and basement boutiques selling vinyl records and the second-hand clothes Rachel liked to wear. Elm trees fronted the brick and granite buildings and flower baskets hung from refurbished nineteenth-century gaslights. Across the street was a millrace, overhung with willows. In good weather, college students sat on the grass verge between the sidewalk and the water, smoking, playing guitars, making out, drinking beer if they could get away with it.

Coming out of the music store, squinting at these students in the sunlight, Tariq felt as if they lived a life of freedom he would never know.

It was his first time out of the house since the incident. This street was the last place Brad and his friends would frequent, but the breadth of vista, the noisy traffic, and the open air brought on a fluttering near Tariq's heart and a sickening twinge in his gut. As if he were waiting to be struck. Hugging the buildings, he made his way under the awnings to the converted bank that was now a Starbucks franchise. But he was a half hour early for Rachel, so he crossed the street and ducked into one of the funky record stores to escape the light and to see if he could find 'Impressions'.

That morning he had looked up John Coltrane on Wikipedia. A photograph showed a middle-aged black man in a white open-necked shirt and a striped suit jacket several sizes too small.

His saxophone hung from its neck strap as if part of his body, and he stared off-camera with eyes locked with intensity. Tariq read, to his surprise, that Coltrane had died forty-five years ago. The tune on the radio had sounded as if written yesterday. And he *was* a religious figure. A saint in the African Orthodox Church, beatified five years after his death.

On YouTube there had been no 'Impressions', but plenty else by Coltrane: 'Blue Train' and 'Alabama' and 'Giants Steps'. Tariq listened to them all. None had the anguish of 'Impressions,' but all had that tone that made Tariq's insides vibrate like a reed in the wind. The music was like *choubi*, but new and different.

The record store was cramped and badly lit and smelled of incense. From the rear a deep voice boomed: 'Shit. Ain't heard nothing that wild since Miles played in Japan.' A crackle of laughter, then a frantic piece of electric jazz exploding from ceiling speakers before the volume was lowered. Eyes adjusting to the light, Tariq walked between the rows of old records. Two men leaned on opposite sides of a counter at the back of the shop. The customer was a white guy with long grey hair and shabby clothes. The counter assistant was a tall black man with a shaved head and an earring that shone in the gloom like the morning star.

Tariq had no way of playing vinyl, but there were only records in the aisles. No CDs. No cassette tapes. A lot of jazz, though, and a Coltrane section that was deep and varied. As he looked through the selection, the grey-haired man squeezed past him, smelling like the homeless who slept in doorways on Harbour Road.

'Something in particular you looking for?'

The other man had come out from behind the counter. He was huge. What's more, he only had one arm and wore a long African robe, quite like his father's prayer gown, but decorated with intricate rows of embroidery in green, red and yellow. His perfectly bald head gleamed beneath the fluorescent light.

Tariq stared. The man grinned maniacally, flashing a gold tooth. He had a wispy goatee and a nasty scar that ran from the base of his neck into the folds of the gown. 'Ain't gonna bite you, my man. Can't tell you what we got till you tell me what you want.'

'Do you have any CDs?'

'I got a few.'

'I'm looking for "Impressions", by –'

'*Trane!*' the man shouted, without warning. 'JC, Jesus Christ, Mister John Col*trane!*'

He closed his eyes, raised his lone arm and swayed back and forth, as if listening to some inner cosmic music.

When Tariq said nothing, the man opened his eyes and glared at him fiercely with a face like an African mask. The goatee quivered. '*I start in the middle of a sentence and move both directions at once.* You know who said that?'

'John Coltrane?'

'My *man!*'

He raised his hand, looking for a high-five. His fingers were long and crooked. Tariq gave them a tentative pat.

The man edged him aside and flipped one-handed through the Coltrane records. He was at least a foot taller than Tariq and broad across the shoulders. Lithe and muscular, like a cheetah. The empty sleeve of his gown flapped as he worked through the stack. 'You looking for the album,' he said, 'or just the tune?'

'Album?'

He slapped a faded sleeve on top of one of the rows. '*Impressions*, Impulse Records, 1963. Recorded live at the Village Vanguard in New York City.' His deep voice shimmered with the pride of someone who knows a subject well. The record had a price tag of thirty-five dollars and featured a picture of Coltrane, face creased in concentration, playing a soprano saxophone. 'Original sleeve. First edition. Third cut is the *tune* "Impressions".'

'The tune, I guess. I heard it on the radio yesterday.'

'And you dug it.'

'Well, I liked it. Yeah.'

'You don't *like* Trane, my man, you *live* him, know what I'm saying? You play?'

By now, Tariq was answering questions just to get the conversation over with. The man's bristling energy and edgy voice were too much. Especially in such a small dark space.

'Clarinet,' Tariq said.

'You dig John Carter? Don Byron?'

'I don't really play jazz.'

'Don't *really* play it?'

'I play classical.'

The man slid a second record from the bin. His single hand was quick and dexterous, like a magician's.

'OK, check this out. First album is pricey, I give you that. But if it's the tune you're looking for, then it's also on this re-release.' He tapped the record. 'Same cut, plus other great shit: "Spiritual", "Chasin' the Trane", "Softly, As in a Morning Sunrise". This one I can give you for eight bucks.'

'I don't have a record-player. Do you have it on CD?'

'Can't play vinyl? What I always say: the young people of today. But, hey, no problem, I can put it on order for you.'

'How much?'

'Can't say exactly, but I won't charge you more than ten bucks. Guaranteed.'

The man's wide eyes were bloodshot, his bared teeth yellow.

'OK, I guess,' Tariq said.

The man returned to his place behind the counter and took an index card and stubby pencil from a drawer. 'What's your name?'

'Tariq. Tariq Mussam.'

The guy raised his eyebrows and Tariq spelled it.

'You got a telephone number, Tariq?'

He gave him his cell number. The man wrote it carefully beside his name and slipped the index card into a plastic pouch beside the cash register. 'Week or so. I'll give you a call.'

'Thanks,' Tariq said. 'I have to go.'

When he was halfway down the aisle, the man shouted. 'Hey. Tell me this. Where you from?'

Tariq paused before answering. 'Monroe,' he said.

The man considered this response. 'Born and raised?'

'I was born in Baghdad. In Iraq.'

The man narrowed his eyes. The half of his body visible above the counter appeared to grow even bigger, and Tariq's gaze was drawn to the space where his right arm should have been and the way the loose sleeve moved like a flag in a light breeze.

'Baghdad,' the man said, so softly that Tariq barely heard. 'I know where Baghdad is.'

AT the back of Starbucks was an alcove of easy chairs, low tables and, on sunny days, shafts of mote-filled light that pillared from a pair of skylights high above. It was Rachel's favourite place to hang out. She sat on the edge of her chair, huddled over a latte, her tangled hair gathered in an unruly ponytail. Opposite her, one leg sprawled over the chair arm, was her friend Annalise, who stared into space while Rachel chatted non-stop. When she saw Tariq, Rachel put down her cup, struck a sexy pose, and tapped out an awkward rhythm with a pair of brass finger cymbals.

'What do you think?' she said.

'Think of what?'

She shook the cymbals. 'Aren't these perfect for your music?'

'I don't know.'

'Tariq, c'mon. You're the expert.'

'I don't think they use those for Iraqi dance. More Egyptian. You know, belly-dancers.'

Annalise guffawed. She was a senior who worked on the school paper with Rachel, wore sunglasses in all weathers and liked to smoke weed. Jewish, like Rachel, but without the consciousness. She wasn't unfriendly, but Tariq never felt comfortable with her stoner comments and biker-girl pose. And her presence dulled Rachel's usual sharpness.

'That's what they mean by "suitable attire",' Annalise said. 'Show some flesh and shake your *thang*, girl.'

Tariq sat in a third chair. The leather was warm from the sunlight.

'You getting some coffee?' Rachel said.

He grimaced.

'Oh, I forgot.' She said to Annalise. 'It's Ramadan.'

'Rama-lama-ding-dong,' Annalise said, sputtering into laughter. She was definitely high.

The place was half-full, most of the patrons college kids with laptops, knapsacks and sleepy eyes. Kids a million miles from Brad's outlook but alien to Tariq as well. Who took five minutes to decide what they wanted to drink and talked about eco-friendly career choices and the best graduate schools. Kids Rachel made fun of, except when she was here.

'We saw you outside,' Annalise said, 'like, half an hour ago.'

'Yeah, you walked right by. Where did you go?'

'You said two o'clock. So I went to a record store. Across the street.'

'Not the Jazz Dungeon,' Annalise said.

'Yeah.'

'So you met Jamal the psycho.'

'I don't know who I met.'

'Big black guy? One arm?'

Tariq nodded.

'Then you met him. *Nobody* goes in there. Psycho weird music and mega-weird guy behind the counter.'

'His name's Jamal?'

Annalise stood and yawned and stretched her arms high so that the hem of her sweatshirt lifted, exposing a mound of taut belly above the waist of her low jeans and a silver stud nestled in the bud of her navel.

'I gotta scoot,' she said.

'Hey,' Rachel said to her, ringing the cymbals, 'first class tonight. You should come.'

'No can do.'

'Tariq doesn't know it, but he's our special guest.'

'Oh, you gonna play that snake-charmer shit?' Annalise said.

'I don't think so,' Tariq said. He was eager for Annalise to be gone, but worried as well.

'You could be, like, the pied piper. All the girls following you to your cave.'

Rachel laughed and stood up, and the girls hugged.

'See you later, Sinbad,' Annalise said to Tariq, touching his nose.

He watched her as she walked away. The way she moved her hips in her tight, frayed jeans would have enraged his father.

'What was that all about?' he said. 'Pied piper?'

'She thinks you're cute.'

She meant, '*I* think you're cute.' He could smile. He could tell her *she* was cute. Instead he scowled and his face grew hot. 'And *Sinbad*? Kind of racist, don't you think?'

'Oh, c'mon. It's all about context.'

'What's her context?'

'Attraction. In this instance.'

'Getting baked, more like. Getting high and saying stupid things.'

That morning, Tariq had watched the news on Al Jazeera with his parents. They had the channel on their satellite package. Iraq had returned to the centre of attention. Suicide bombers. Shias and Sunnis killing each other. Kids like himself waving banners and throwing stones. Desert, oil, Islam.

For once, Tariq felt more at home with his parents and their Arabic obsession than he did outside the house. Even the mosque last night, when his father had forced him to go, was soothing. The murmured prayers, the way everyone bowed together, the imam's monotonous voice. Tariq did not stand out there. He did not grow embarrassed when girls touched him. He was not scared that kids would throw rocks at him or humiliate him because of where he was from. Sitting beside his mother on the couch had been comforting. To stay at home, surrounded by the lacquered boxes and fat pillows and brass trays, was so tempting. Ride the lonely ship at sea. Rachel was Monday, the return to school, the American reality of difference.

But she was his secret desire. And she was always sending him encouraging messages.

So why couldn't he tell her how he felt?

With Annalise gone, Rachel had grown serious. 'You worry about racism?' she said.

'You don't?'

'God, no. My parents do that for me. *B'nai B'rith*, the ADL. Card-carrying members. Racism's all they think about.'

'It's different for us.'

'Ah. For us. For the *Arabs*.'

43

She gave him that look. That *don't-pull-this-shit* look. There is no hierarchy of suffering, she liked to say. And when she said it, he would change the subject. Because, to be honest, when she got her mind going in that direction, he couldn't follow her.

'You know what they say,' he ventured, watching her eyes.

'Who?'

'Kids at school.'

Her expression softened. 'I know. But those guys are stupid. And easy to deal with. The right word with Mr Higgins and you could get that Jorgensen dickhead expelled.'

He moved out of the sunlight and into another chair. He was hot. Short of breath.

'What happened on Thursday?' she said.

'Is that why you wanted to meet? To ask me that?'

She touched his hand. 'Hey, no. To see you. To tell you about the dance class.'

'What did you hear?'

She folded her hands on her lap. Her glasses had slipped to the end of her nose. 'That they pushed you around in the parking lot.'

He stared at the table. 'Is that all?'

'What else is there?'

'Nothing.'

'Did they hurt you?'

'*No.*'

'Why weren't you in school yesterday?'

'I was *sick*. I *told* you.'

Absent-mindedly, she pushed her glasses up the bridge of her nose and undid her ponytail. Her dark hair fell over her shoulders. Her mouth was tight, her eyes shifting, as if she wanted to say something but was holding back. And he could say nothing. He felt closest to her when she seemed most distant from him.

44

She had asked to meet, and when the moment for real talk arrived, he had clammed up.

She picked up the finger cymbals from the table, put them in her bag, took out a folder and handed it to him.

'What's this?' he said.

'English homework. And history.'

'Right. Thanks.'

'I better get ready for my dance class.'

'OK.'

Above them a pigeon landed on the skylight glass with a flurry of flapping wings and scrabbling talons. Its movement cast a dancing shadow on the table between them.

As they stood outside the coffee shop, preparing to part, she grasped his arm above the elbow. 'I'll meet you near the gas station on Monday morning,' she said. 'We can walk into school together.'

'Why?'

'Just so we can.'

Chapter 5

CONGREGANTS filed into the mosque for evening prayers on Saturday, deeply uneasy. Women looked at the ground, men avoided each other's eyes, families dropped their voices to a whisper long before reaching the prayer hall. Late that afternoon, word had spread that the body of Anat Hassan, wife of a prominent Egyptian businessman in the town, had been found on an isolated stretch of lakefront near the old Harbinger Hotel. She had been missing for two days, and the police were not looking for suspects.

Like blank pages, three unoccupied prayer rugs lay where Mr Hassan and his young sons usually knelt. When it came time for Imam Mohammad to speak, he stayed silent for a long time, touching his forehead with two fingers, before quoting the Qur'an: *Do not throw yourselves into destruction.* He said in a soft but firm voice that he who commits suicide must face eternal damnation, where he will experience the manner of his death repeatedly, without end.

So if you shot yourself in the mouth, Tariq reasoned as he listened, in hell you would be shot in the mouth over and over again. For ever. How could that be?

His mother had told him that Mrs Hassan was asked to leave Cloverleaf Mall last year after flapping the arms of her cloak beside a play area for children and screaming in Arabic at the young mothers. Nobody knew what she had said, Zaida insisted, but after a soccer match in Gibson Field, Ali Farouk had told Tariq and other boys that she had called the mothers whores and told them they would roast in hell. Whatever she had said, the fear in her heart had finally brought her to the edge of Lake Verona, where she chose the largest stones that would fit in her pockets before walking into the deep. So that now, as Imam Mohammad claimed, she would be forbidden the fruits of paradise. Tariq thought of her two boys, who attended a private elementary school on the other side of Monroe. Of what they were doing at that moment, instead of attending Saturday prayers. Of what they would feel the first time their father made them return to mosque.

'There is no god but Allah,' the imam concluded, 'the Forbearing, the Generous. There is no god but Allah, the Eminent, the Great. Glory be to Allah, the sustainer of the seven heavens and of the seven earths, the sustainer of all the things in them, and between them, the Lord of the great Throne.'

When the prayers were over, Tariq and his father waited on the hall steps for his mother to join them from the mosque kitchen. His Uncle Rahim limped over to say hello and await an invitation to the evening meal. His big body swayed heavily as he moved, his gown tight on his thick frame, his skullcap askew.

Tariq's uncle was so different from Malik that even people who had known them both for years marvelled that they were brothers. Rahim was barrel-chested, broad-faced and happy-go-lucky, with an unkempt beard and eyes that glimmered with emotion. He was an auto mechanic, a gambler, a singer and a master of the oud. He could play any Iraqi tune requested, and transcribed *maqam* and *choubi* in a notebook bound in the same leather as the journal he had given Tariq.

Tariq and his family had left Iraq several years before the American invasion. Rahim chose to remain in Baghdad, and after the fall of Saddam Hussein he was rewarded for his loyalty with seven days of torture in the basement of an old factory in al-Jadriya, not three blocks from the house where Tariq had been born and where Rahim had still lived with his family. Shia guards from the Interior Ministry threatened to fetch his wife and her sister and rape them in front of him. He was deprived of food for a week and shocked with electric wires. The guards had burned him with their cigarettes; the scars were pink and shiny and scattered on his hands and neck like splattered raindrops. Ever since, he had walked with a limp.

'The imam wasn't pulling punches, was he?' Rahim said to Malik. 'He was teaching.'

'He doesn't like Hassan any more than the rest of us.'

'Keep your voice down.' Malik glanced over his shoulder. 'Don't let Zaida hear you say that. Speaking ill of the dead.'

Rahim had a fit of coughing. Waved a finger. 'I'm not referring to that poor woman. It's that dog of a husband, with his fat arse and his Cadillac Escalade.'

Malik shrugged. 'What do you care about Sadiki Hassan and his fancy cars?'

'What do I care? That he still owes me four hundred dollars for installing a transmission. That he accuses me of overcharging, when he's the biggest thief in the city.'

Rahim turned to Tariq and said in English, 'Rickey, have you been practising my songs?'

Rickey was his uncle's pet name for him. No-one else called him that.

'He's preparing for the school concert,' Malik said. 'He doesn't have time for such nonsense.'

Rahim winked at Tariq. It was as if the conversation about Hassan had not taken place. 'Your baba is ashamed of his own music.'

'I am not.'

'What is John Philip Sousa compared to the wonders of *choubi*?'

'He plays Brahms. Mozart.'

'And your songs, Uncle,' Tariq said quietly.

Rahim hummed the melody to 'Oh, People of Reason', keeping time by slapping his thigh with his hand. Malik shuffled in place, irritated. As he finished, Zaida approached in her best silk robe and blue hijab.

'What nightclub music are you teaching my son now, Rahim?' she said, her tone playful.

Rahim smiled and bowed. 'I could tell your son stories, Zaida. The book market on Mutanabbi Street. Playing oud beneath the palm trees beside the river. Going to the clubs in Adhamiyah.'

'I hear the clubs are dead,' Zaida said. 'Since the ban on alcohol.'

Rahim scoffed and waved his hand as if clearing cobwebs from the air. 'Zealots. Fanatics who would kill our culture.'

'Alcohol is the least of their worries,' Malik said. 'We should thank Allah we live where we do.'

Zaida looped her arm through Tariq's. 'Are you hungry, *habibi*?'

He disengaged and moved away from her. She raised her eyebrows to Rahim, who removed his skullcap and ran his fingers through his thick hair. 'If you want to thank Allah, Malik, make thanks that your wife is such a fine cook.' He asked her, 'Is there room at the table for a hungry cripple?'

'You are always welcome, Rahim.'

'Good. Because I could eat a camel.'

THE car was quiet on their way home. Malik drove slowly through the dark streets, and Zaida stared out the window, fingering the hem of her hijab. Sleepy from the big meal, Tariq slumped in the back, listening to the wind rush through the open windows. The night sky was clear, and the blinking lights of a descending aircraft tracked the car as it passed through the empty business district.

As they idled at a red light, Tariq's mother said, as if to herself, 'Anat made flat bread last year for Eid al-Adha. And date bread.'

'Anat?' Malik said.

Zaida kept staring out the window. 'Anat Hassan.'

Into the silence that followed came the rumble of a muscle car, which pulled up beside them at the lights. Full of high-school boys, it thumped with loud music and drunken revelry. Before he could see who they were, Tariq slouched further in his seat, so that his eyes were below the level of the window.

But one of the boys had seen him and was shouting. Tariq looked straight ahead. Another boy said something to Zaida. Because of the music, it was impossible to understand the words, but the tone was clear.

'*What* did he say?' Malik said.

Zaida rolled up her window. 'Ignore them.'

'Filthy beasts,' Malik said, opening the car door and getting out.

But the light had changed and the muscle car fish-tailed away with a squeal of rubber. An arm extended from the rear window and tossed a beer bottle high in the air. It smashed on the hood of the Mussams' car, and Tariq shouted in fright.

'Animals,' Malik yelled. He got back in, slamming the door and thrusting the car into gear. In his agitation, he stalled the engine. He ranted in Arabic.

'Calm down,' Zaida said, touching his arm. 'They are gone.'

'Of course they are gone! Getting away with behaviour like that. It should not be allowed. It should be reported.'

Again Malik tried to start the car, but the engine had flooded.

He stared at the tail-lights tunnelling into the distance. He gripped the steering wheel so hard his hands were white.

Exhaling loudly, he turned and leaned over the seat. 'Those boys,' he said to Tariq, 'who are they?'

'How would I know?'

'They knew you.'

'No. They did not.'

Malik glared at him.

'I never saw them before,' Tariq said.

IN bed that night Tariq was aware of every small sound: water coursing through the pipes, the rustle of the trees, the Greenbriars' air conditioner going off and on, the swish of distant traffic. In Baghdad, when gunfire had sounded in the street below their window, he had his mother and father in the same bed with him, his uncle and aunt in the next room. Here in peaceful suburban Monroe he was on his own, and the simplest of night sounds had become more disturbing than the terrors of war.

Rahim had been abducted six years ago, when Tariq was eleven. His wife, Leyla, assumed he had been killed. Every day of the week he was missing she had been on the phone to Tariq's parents, wailing, pleading, threatening to do away with herself. She called at nine AM – five in the afternoon in Baghdad – as soon as she had returned from her day-long vigil outside the offices of the Interior Ministry. They told her nothing until the sixth day. By then, Malik had made arrangements to take leave from Monroe General and that morning had bought a plane ticket home. Home. That was how he had put it to Zaida.

He did not go. Rahim was in bad shape but defiant. He spoke to Malik by phone from Ibn Sina Hospital, where he was being treated by American doctors. 'Leyla and I are coming to the US,' he said. 'This is the final straw. The pigs running the country are worse than Saddam ever was. Make the arrangements.'

Because of his history, it was possible for Rahim to get refugee status, and six months after being released from hospital he and Leyla flew to Chicago with their green cards. Malik, Zaida and Tariq met them at O'Hare, and they drove to Monroe through a blizzard. They lived in the Mussam house for nearly a year, and it was like the old times. For Tariq, anyhow. Rahim played the oud and transcribed songs. Leyla sang *maqam* and recited classical Arabic poetry. The house rang with music.

In the first months of that year, the brothers sat in the kitchen late every night, Rahim drinking *arak*, Malik mint tea. Tariq heard their voices percolate through the floorboards, his father's even and murmuring, Rahim's swooping and dramatic. Occasionally a word would break free into coherence: *haqq*, *adl*, *azaab*.

Tariq recognised these words from his study of the Qur'an: truth, justice, torture.

'What was it like?' he once asked his uncle, as they took a break from playing *choubi* in Tariq's room.

'In al-Jadriya?'

Tariq nodded.

'The more they hurt me, the stronger I became. When that Shia dog broke my leg I spat in his face.'

'Were you afraid?'

Rahim examined his fingers resting on the strings of the oud.

'Listen to this, Rickey.' He played a chord. 'I want you to play the melody *through* that sound, do you understand? Like wind through the trees.'

How could a man come out of a torture cell in the rubble of Baghdad with a smile and a song, while Mrs Hassan, with her money and clothes and big house in the richest place on earth, could not face another day of her life?

It was hours before Tariq fell asleep.

Chapter 6

TARIQ sat at the back of English class, monitoring the body language of those in the desks ahead: the boys loose and sprawling, the girls upright and attentive. Heavily pregnant, her bright orange hair teased into a woolly mass, Ms Berman waddled around the classroom, reciting lines from *Hamlet* and springing pointed questions on the unsuspecting. Tariq tried hard to stay alert. He had read the passage for the day. He had prepared answers to the assigned questions. But his thoughts were like stalks of straw in a tornado.

He had logged on to Facebook before school. On his page, someone had left a link to a 'Like' page with the legend: *That awkward moment when they serve pork chops in the cafeteria.* The picture on the page was one of Tariq and Yusef, taken on Diversity Day last year. They were both scowling. Already, forty-seven people 'liked' the page. There was one anonymous comment. *What a freak show.*

He had moved through the morning like a soldier on patrol, heart thudding, palms damp, fearful of ambush at every corner. In home room, the other students were both friendlier and more distant than usual, smiling too broadly while avoiding eye contact. Rachel claimed he was imagining things, and it was true that he was hyper-aware of his surroundings, the hallway thunder between classes, the smells of floor wax and bubblegum and overheated bodies, the squeak of sneakers on linoleum as students milled from room to room. Class was a haven, but temporary; the clock above each teacher's head ticked like a bomb; the sound of the bell was like a smashed plate.

'It's like the most clichéd speech in *all* of Shakespeare,' Amy Zelensky said. One of Ms Berman's pets, she sat in the front row. Rachel hated her.

'This coming from the girl who has read all thirty-seven plays,' Ms Berman said. 'It is thirty-seven, isn't it, Amy? Do we count *The Two Noble Kinsmen?*'

'You know what I mean. "To be or not to be, that is the question".'

'Keep going.'

Amy's head stiffened as she searched for the words.

'Yadda, yadda, yadda,' Shawn Benson said, and everyone laughed.

Amy did not look back. '*Whether 'tis nobler in the mind to ...*' She waved a hand in defeat. 'Oh, you know, like, sea of troubles and so on.'

'Care to complete the soliloquy, Shawn?' Ms Berman said.

'I just did.'

With a withering look, Ms Berman recited the next ten lines or so, putting on an English accent and rolling her r's theatrically.

She paused and turned to Amy. 'It may be the most familiar *line*.'

'That's what I meant.'

'Even then, familiarity does not make it a cliché. It's like arguing that creating Shylock makes Shakespeare anti-Semitic.'

Outside, a car roared past, radio blaring. The heat had persisted. Sounds of freedom flowed through the open windows: birdsong, distant laughter, the ceaseless whine of the crickets.

'Tariq,' Ms Berman said.

He sat up. The class's attention funnelled back to him.

'This speech is a soliloquy. Do you agree?'

'Uh, yes.'

'Why?'

He shrugged. 'Because he's speaking to the audience?'

'Even though Ophelia is standing nearby? Couldn't he be speaking to her?'

'I don't know. I guess.'

'At any rate, a soliloquy allows us to see into the mind of the character,' Ms Berman said. 'To hear what he is thinking.'

'Yeah.'

'So what is he thinking?'

Tariq's face was hot. He focused on the teacher's halo of orange hair but felt the eyes of the class on him.

'Whether to ... you know, kill himself,' he said.

'And what does he decide?'

'He doesn't. Basically, he's a guy who can't decide. Who can't make up his mind about anything. Killing himself. Killing the king.'

'And why does he want to kill himself?'

He searched for words. It was as if a huge weight hung above him, about to fall.

'I'm not sure that he does.'

'Ah.'

Rachel sat halfway up the class, in the same row as Tariq. Though he felt her scrutiny, he could not look her way. Yet he knew she was about to speak.

'Maybe,' Rachel said, 'that's what he wants Ophelia to believe. What he wants her to *think* he's thinking. And that's what puts the idea of, you know, suicide into *her* head. Another of his mistakes. Talking so loosely about such a serious issue.'

Ms Berman looked from Rachel to Tariq and back again. She nodded and stiffly moved back to her desk and took the line of questioning in a different direction.

After class, Rachel waited for him in the hall.

'Hey.'

'Aren't you going to lunch?' he said.

'I'm not hungry. Thought I'd listen to you practise.'

She had met him near the gas station that morning as arranged. They had walked in silence until, near the school doors, he'd asked her if she'd been on Facebook that day. She admitted she had.

'I'd rather be by myself,' he said to her now.

'OK,' she said. 'Are you sure?'

'Yes.'

'Because I don't mind hanging out with you.'

'I'm sure.'

She made no move to leave. He scanned the faces of the kids streaming down the hallway. They were tense with the pent-up energy of a long hot morning of classes. This release and the smell of impure cafeteria food led them on, like animals to the trough.

When the crowd had thinned, she said, 'You could say something.'

'To who?'

'Like we talked about.'

'No.'

'Idiots post these things, Tariq. They have no idea that they might be hurting other people. You need to say something.'

'No. Too much has been said already. I have to go.'

He left her standing in the hall and got his clarinet and went to the band room, but as soon as he was inside he grew nervous. It was the first time all day he had been by himself. He left his clarinet in the room and walked to the end of the hallway and up the south stairwell. On the third-floor landing was an alcove that looked down on the school's rear entrance. He would hear anyone coming up the stairs long before they would see him.

He sat in the alcove and stared out the window. To the left was the parking lot. To the right, beyond the crowns of the swaying cottonwoods, the football field. The field was empty, and on its surrounding all-weather track was a lone runner. Sunlight glinted off the goal posts. It was a picture a yearbook editor would love, an early autumn scene of tranquillity perfect as filler between class photos.

But the parking lot tugged at his attention. The area where he'd been assaulted, maze-like with painted arrows and angled spaces, was empty. With a shudder he realised that the girls who had looked down at him on Thursday had been standing right here, in the alcove. They'd had an aerial view of his torment as he lay on the tarmac, his school things scattered like dead leaves, his bare flesh on full display. From up here his frantic flailing and shouts in Arabic would have appeared like the efforts of a trapped mouse. Were they shocked or amused? Did it matter?

Without warning the hall door beside him flew open, and Yusef jogged through, stopping in surprise when he saw Tariq. He had forgotten that the physics and chemistry labs were on this floor and that Yusef would be up here at lunchtime.

'What are you doing?' Yusef said.

'Nothing.'

'We're supposed to be working. Not wandering the hallways. If Higgins sees you we could both get detention.'

'Don't worry. I'm not going to get you in trouble.'

Though the school did not allow facial hair, Yusef had permission for religious reasons to wear a beard. Ragged and sparse, it elongated his already thin face, with its mournful, hooded eyes and dramatic hooked nose. Tariq had yet to start shaving. Yusef wore the same outfit every day: black pants, black leather shoes and a crisp white shirt, always freshly ironed. Rachel called him Rasputin.

Tariq waited for him to go, but Yusef set his schoolbag on the floor and stood with his hands folded at his chest like an imam. Had he seen the Facebook page?

'I heard what happened last week,' he said.

Tariq said nothing.

'Everyone knows,' Yusef said.

'I don't believe that. Nobody has said anything to me. Except you.'

Yusef waved his hand and frowned. 'You think that means they're not saying anything to each other? These people don't know the Qur'an. *Do not spy and do not backbite one another.* Loose people have loose tongues.'

'Well, I don't care what they think.'

'So it's true.'

'It's none of your business.'

Yusef stroked his beard, as if tugging on it might produce wisdom.

'Those boys should be punished,' Yusef pronounced. 'Otherwise they will do it again.'

'I told you. It's none of your business. I'm not talking to you about it.'

'Are you talking to your Jewish friends about it?'

'My *Jewish* friends?'

'Do you really think it's healthy to be spending time with girls who are racist? Who look down on people like us.'

'Who exactly are you talking about?'

'Throughout history, Jews have harassed us and plotted against anyone who believes in Muhammad.'

Tariq looked out the window. 'Leave me alone, Yusef.'

Yusef picked up his bag. 'At some point you'll realise that you can't depend on anyone but your own. Think about it. Who else understands? They tell us they accept us and want us to be part of their culture. Then they spit on our beliefs and tell us that *we're* intolerant. You have to stand up to the boys who did this to you. And reporting them won't do any good. Go to your own people. You can't let this happen.'

'I'm not going to anyone. Just leave me alone.'

'You can't let this happen, Tariq.'

'I said leave me *alone*.'

Yusef shrugged, slung the bag over his shoulder and went down the stairs.

THE last period of the day would be gym. Sitting in history class, counting down the minutes, Tariq's palms grew clammy, his stomach nauseous. He was so inattentive that Mr Allen finally asked him what was wrong.

'I don't feel well.'

'Do you need to see the nurse?'

'Yes, I do.'

The school nurse excused him from gym class, and he felt better at once. Still, he lay on the couch in her office for the whole period, listening to the college radio station while she filled out forms and asked him about Islam. He had told her it was probably the fasting that had made him ill.

The final bell sounded. The nurse did not rush him but after another twenty minutes asked if she should phone his parents. He told her they were both working. She said that she had to close the infirmary and that she could, if he liked, arrange a taxi to pick him up. He thought about what his father would say if he found out that he had taken a cab home, and he told the nurse that he was feeling better.

The halls were empty. He decided that the best route home was the most trafficked, and he left the school by the front door.

As soon as he was outside, Brad Jorgensen stepped out from behind a pillar and blocked his way, one foot set at the base of the door so that Tariq could not go back inside. He was so close that

Tariq could see the individual hairs of his stubble and the jagged lines of the lightning bolt tattoo on his neck. He leaned back, pushing his shoulder blades against the glass door. Over Brad's shoulder, two girls on rollerblades swept past, long hair streaming in the wind.

'Don't worry,' Brad said, 'I'm not going to touch you.'

Tariq was not convinced. He looked at the ground. The frayed cuffs of Brad's jeans loosely overlapped oil-stained work boots.

'Who'd you tell?'

'Nobody,' Tariq said.

'Bull*shit*.'

Head down, Tariq spread his hands. He felt Brad's warm breath on his forehead. 'I haven't said a word to anyone. I know you don't believe me, but it's a fact.'

Brad stuck a finger under Tariq's chin and pushed his head up so that they were eye to eye. 'So how does everyone know? What's this shit I hear about you being on the Internet?'

'Maybe somebody saw.'

An animal flicker in Brad's eye said that he was scared. But that didn't make Tariq feel any safer.

'It's not like we hurt you or anything. So you got pantsed. Big fucking deal. You so much of a wuss you're gonna go squeal to mama?'

'I told you, I didn't tell anyone.'

Brad stepped back. He held his arms loose but ready at his side, like a fighter. The hunch of his shoulders and the twisted line of his mouth announced his grievance. Tariq knew the body language. A lot of kids on the west side had it. Pinched and tawdry and defensive, like the duplexes and bungalows they lived in with their dark, dirty windows and yards littered with old tyres and broken toys.

Brad dropped his voice. His fingers curled, almost into fists, as he spoke. 'Yeah, well, if you do, so help you God. Because you would so regret it. Because you have no fucking idea.'

He hitched his shoulders, spat on the ground and drifted backwards, his boots scraping the sidewalk. For once he had spoken without bravado or disdain, and as he walked away Tariq saw the fear in his gait and knew that such fear was far more dangerous than insults about prayer and taunts from the vacant lot.

When he reached the street, Brad looked back over his shoulder and pointed at his own eyes with two fingers. Tariq had no idea what it meant.

Chapter 7

TARIQ stood at the rear of the hall, in shadow, watching the dancers move through their routines at the brighter end. They performed in front of a long mirror bisected by a wooden rail, and their doubled bodies moved in time to a song coming from a portable CD player in the corner. The music was generic and pedestrian: Turkish or Lebanese pop, to his ear.

The instructor and the dancers were all women, except for a tall man in a tank top. Rachel was on the far left, wearing a headscarf, a long loose red T-shirt, black leggings and ballet slippers. She did not know Tariq was there. Her arms moved like plants underwater. Her hips swayed to the Arabic beat. She danced with her eyes closed and her mouth half-open in the ecstatic expression he knew so well from her displays in the band room.

But she had learned. Her movement was more natural and fluid. There was an elegant pattern. And she was the least self-conscious of them all, grooving to the tune in her own internal space. Seeing her move like this made Tariq wish he had his clarinet with him. His Uncle Rahim's music would accompany her graceful dance so much better than these tinny songs. And playing might have released him from the numbness he had felt all morning.

'Shoulders high,' the instructor shouted above the music, 'and head still. Let the hips do the work. Very good, Rachel.'

It was noon on Saturday. He had walked to the dance studio from the university through a fine fall day. College students swarmed the streets. Traffic was heavier. The summer heat had lifted, there was a bite in the air and the sky's vault was deep and blue. But he had risen from bed that morning sleepy and disoriented. Ramadan was over and the sight of his parents at the breakfast table in daylight was strange. During the week, the mosque had celebrated Eid-ul-Fitr with several long prayer services and large feasts. For three days Tariq had been excused from school. His parents had also taken time off from their jobs, so both were going to work this Saturday. Tariq was expected to study for the weekend.

His father had greeted him as he entered the kitchen: '*Eid Mubarak.*'

Tariq did not answer. He poured himself a bowl of cereal and sat at the table. His parents were eating fried eggs and peppers.

'So now you are allowed to eat, and this is what you prepare for yourself?' Malik said.

'It's what I like.'

'Worthless.' Malik pointed at the cereal box and said to Zaida, 'Why do you buy this trash?'

She did not answer but said to Tariq, 'What are you doing today?'

'He's studying,' Malik said.

'I know that. Where are you studying? At school?'

'School is closed,' Tariq said.

'I thought the resource centre was open on Saturday.'

'I brought my books home. I'll work here.'

Malik had finished his food and pushed the plate aside. His upper lip bulged where his tongue worked at a bit of food between his teeth. There was a small grease stain on his suit jacket, just above the range of pens in the coat pocket. 'We all have to be home at six,' he said, 'to get ready for prayers.'

Tariq groaned.

'And what is that animal sound supposed to signify?' his father said.

'You're going to mosque *again?*'

'We are all going. It is Saturday.'

'Well, I'll say my prayers at home today,' Tariq said.

'Of course you will. And you will come to mosque for *maghrib*. As it says in the Qur'an: *The virtuous are those who keep their pledges.* You will come for your sake and for the sake of the family.'

'No. I won't. I told you, I'm not going.'

Malik leaned on his elbows and smiled. 'Big man. Big decisions.'

'It's not obligatory,' Tariq said. 'Isn't that right, Ommi?'

As he looked at his mother his father slapped him on the side of the head, hard. Tariq's chest bumped his bowl, spilling milk and cereal onto the table. Through the pain and buzz in his ear he heard his mother shouting in Arabic. Dizzy and near tears, he pushed his chair over and lashed out at the overturned bowl so that it spun across the table and smashed on the tiled floor. His parents were standing and yelling, at each other and at him, and he rushed to his room. But the chaos in his head was no less upstairs, and the walls of his bedroom moved in and out to the throbbing in his ear, so he grabbed his jacket and returned downstairs and left the house. As he ran across the front grass he heard his mother cry out from the doorway, but he did not look back until he was two blocks away.

His phone rang several times as he walked. Knowing that his parents would be driving the main roads to work, he detoured along the side streets, making his way through the adjoining neighbourhoods to the centre of town, past the Whole Foods market, and along the old railway yard to the millrace. He followed the water to the duck pond behind the university, where he sat on one of the benches beneath the shelter of the willows and waited for his heart to calm.

A family of ducks drifted in and out of view. Willow leaves floated on the surface of the water like confetti. At the end of the pond, canoeists paddled by, screened from view by the rushes. He knew that here he would be alone and unobserved.

It was a familiar spot. When his family first moved to Monroe, they would come to this stretch of water for picnics. This was before Tariq knew how to swim. One Sunday, throwing bread crusts to the ducks, he had fallen into the pond. The water was no more than a couple of feet deep, but his mother dove in after him, throwing herself horizontally into the water so that she was fully immersed. She floundered, but clutched Tariq and pushed him towards the bank. His father pulled him from the water and, in one continuous motion, hit him so hard on his bare thigh that Tariq lost his breath.

They didn't yet own a car. Her soaking dress covered in river dirt and dead weeds, Zaida carried a screaming Tariq home. Everyone looked at them. Zaida said nothing and Malik trudged alongside, angry and embarrassed. Once in the house, his parents fought bitterly. Tariq was only five years old at the time, but the day nagged in memory like a toothache.

Years later, they would return on summer days to this same place with friends and relatives, including Leyla and Rahim, who would play his oud and sing softly while Zaida and the other mothers spooned marinated lamb and yogurt onto pita bread and the teen-aged boys slyly watched the college girls in the canoes. Away from the public scrutiny of the other city parks, this sheltered bank was popular with the Iraqis of Monroe, and its willow trees and ducks and cool breezes reminded them of walks along the Tigris in Al Rashid or Salihiya or other Baghdad neighbourhoods. As if remembering Zaida's plunge, Malik was quiet at these gatherings and sat away from the rest of the men, walking the pond banks or reading the Qur'an.

Is that why Tariq had come here today? Because it called to mind his father's discomfort? Because it reminded him of past humiliations, and how they could be overcome? That day he had learned fear. It was a lesson never to be undone. Ever since, the water, its dark depths and surface swirls, threatened and soothed him at the same time.

> it stares at me like a shining fish
>
> telling me to come, come
>
> here to the cool water where all is peace

He finally checked his phone. There were four missed calls from his mother and a text message: *Come to my office at twelve-thirty. We'll have lunch together.*

He called Rachel.

'Are you OK?' she said.

The surface of the pond rippled in the breeze, disturbing the ducks, who flapped and quacked before settling back into their family array. He swallowed and said, 'Do you realise how often you ask me that? Every time I call you, every time we meet in school. "*Are you OK?*"'

'Sorry. Jeez.'

There was a long pause.

'Can you meet me at Starbucks?' he said.

'Now?'

'Yes.'

'I thought you had to study today.'

'Change of plan. Because of my asshole father.'

'*Oh.* What now?'

'I don't want to go into it over the phone.'

'Well, how about lunchtime? After my dance class? I'm getting ready now. Practising.'

She told him the location and the time. He wandered along the millrace, through the university district and past Hawthorne Row. At eleven o'clock he found himself outside his mother's building. He lingered. A small group of students marched past, protesting against Israel. A larger number lay on the grass, reading or sunning themselves.

After a few minutes Tariq went inside and knocked on his mother's office door. She was with a student and asked him to wait. When the student came out, she smiled and stared at him with curiosity.

'You got my text?' Zaida said. 'I said twelve-thirty.'

'I can't make it then.'

'Why?'

'I told Rachel I would go to her dance class.'

His mother nodded, arranging papers on her desktop. It was strange to see her in these surroundings. Though she wore the same clothes as always – silk gown, hijab, low heels – here in the university, with its laid-back energy and bright, resonant hallways and plain furnishings, she looked different. Her caramel-coloured eyes were larger, more alert. Her perfume filled the small room with its sweet odour. She carried herself with professional poise, like an American working woman, confident and in control. Her expression was serious, almost severe.

'I only have a few minutes,' she said. 'I promised I would join the protest.'

'Against Israel?'

'Against their settlements on the West Bank. And East Jerusalem.'

She closed her office door and they sat on opposite sides of her desk. On the bookshelf behind her head were chemistry texts and books of Arabic poetry and political books by Chomsky and Edward Said. A pair of spider plants sat beside ivory bookends. Below them was a picture of Tariq, dressed in a traditional Iraqi *dishdasha*. Thirteen in the photograph, he looked like a different person.

'You worried me,' she said, 'running off like that.'

'What did you expect me to do?'

'Tell your ommi where you were going.' She said this with a light smile and a self-mocking tone. But he knew she was serious.

'I had no choice.'

In front of her was a ceramic vase holding fountain pens, coloured pencils with tasselled eraser caps and a silver letter opener in its sheath. The opener was, he knew, shaped like a sword and decorated with tiny etchings of palm trees, camels and dhows. Her father had given it to her before he died. A bookseller on Mutanabbi Street, he had lost his shop during the Saddam years and died before Tariq was born. He knew that this letter knife was one of his mother's most prized possessions.

'When you run away like that, it makes it more difficult to work things out. Your father had a bad moment. He knew that right away. If you had stayed he would have apologised.'

'He could have phoned me. You called four times.'

'He prefers to speak to you directly.'

'He's never apologised before.'

Zaida took the letter knife from the cup, drew it from its sheath and balanced it in her hand. She had a pained, concentrated expression that made Tariq feel guilty.

'Did he go to work?' Tariq said.

'Yes.'

'So, then. I'll see him tonight. When he gets home from mosque.'

She slid the letter knife back into its sheath. 'This morning, your father did not act like a Muslim,' she said. 'I told him that. But he is going through a difficult time. There are problems at work. People who judge him because of where he's from instead of who he is. I don't think you really understand what a man like him, a proud man, has had to put up with.'

'What about what I have to put up with?'

'You are more at home in Monroe, in this country, than he is. He is an alien here.'

'So are you.'

'The university is different. There are many foreigners on the staff. Foreign students as well. But the hospital...his colleagues are not as open-minded as they could be.'

'Maybe if he wasn't such a religious fanatic.'

She shook her head. 'He practises. As he's been taught.'

'*You* don't.'

He could hear the whine in his voice. He turned panicky as his mother grew calmer. A strange tilting of sympathies was happening. A change.

She brushed the desktop with her palm and said in a tired voice, 'Tariq. *Habibi*. Of course I practise.'

'Not like him.'

'That is one of the glories of Islam. There is no single path.'

'Hitting your son, is that one of the paths? He tells me the virtuous are those who keep their pledges and then he *hits* me?'

'He slapped you. And I told you he regretted that. He knows it was wrong.'

'And is it wrong that he wants you to stay at home and cook and clean? That he's embarrassed because you want to go out and get a job like everybody else in America?'

Her dark eyebrows drew together and she dipped her chin and stared at him. An adult stare that disapproved. Yes, he was losing her. He felt like a small child, about to cry. And he saw that he had come here like a child seeking the comfort she had always given him: a pat on the head, a 'there, there'. But her authority had a new dimension. Maybe it was because they were in her office. Maybe she held him partly responsible for that morning's scene. But everything about her posture and demeanour suggested she was not on his side, as she had ever been.

'Go home and study,' she said. 'And then you will come with us to mosque.'

This command stung as much as his father's slap.

'Because he told me to?' he said. 'Because he hit me?'

'Because it is the right thing to do. Because it is who we are. And next week you will play in this football game, with the Shia madressah. It's been scheduled.'

'I'll think about it.'

'Yes, you'll think about it. That's important. But you'll see that here, too, it is the right thing. You and your father have drifted apart. You need something to bring you close again.'

'And a game of soccer is going to do that?'

'It will do no harm.' She stood up and tapped her watch face. 'My meeting. Are you OK?'

That phrase again, cutting across his despair. 'Yes, yes, I'm *OK*.'

He left the office quickly, before she could come out from behind the desk and kiss him goodbye.

A HALF hour later, watching Rachel move smoothly in the muted light of the studio, Tariq could not scrub his mother's stern expression from his mind. Her hands folded on her desktop. That ridiculous photograph of him over her shoulder. Her hijab shining in the office light.

He had never been able to go against her. So that put him at a disadvantage. He had been ready to stand up to his father, to stay home from prayers and use the morning's slap as a path to the high ground. He was *right*. *He* was the one who had been struck. But his mother, against all his expectation and experience, had undermined him. It was not fair.

Rachel came to the end of her dance with a graceful pivot. More than ever she was someone he wanted to touch and hold. To be close to. In her headscarf and long shirt she did not look Jewish but Middle Eastern. But Jews *were* Middle Eastern, of course.

The music ended and the instructor praised and applauded. The dancers relaxed and mingled. She looked his way but didn't see him; he remained at the dark end of the studio. His palms were damp and his breathing heavy. Partly because of Rachel's dancing and the shape of her figure in the light from the windows. But also because of what his mother had said. She had sabotaged his emotions. He couldn't even trust his own feelings.

And he saw how easy it would be to slide out of the room, under the cover of shadow. Rachel wouldn't even know he'd been there. Because, really, what did he have to say to her? And her to him?

Are you all right?

Chapter 8

TARIQ's phone rang, startling him; he did not remember turning it on. He waited for voicemail to kick in, but the phone kept ringing. A private number. It could be the school, checking up on him. He answered.

Big voice. 'One down, one up.'

'Excuse me?'

A bigger laugh. 'More wisdom from the master.'

Confused, Tariq said nothing.

'Jazz Dungeon here. Your Coltrane order arrived. *Live at the Village Vanguard?*'

'Oh, right. Thanks.'

Tariq was playing his clarinet, as it happened, in his room. He had stayed home sick again from school and his parents were at work. He had forgotten he had ordered the CD. Forgotten about 'Impressions' and that mystical saxophone sound and the strange man in the record store with one arm. Jamal. What had Annalise called him? Jamal the psycho.

'We open till seven you want to pick it up. Every day but Sunday.'

'What about now?'

'Now is good.'

DISSONANT big band jazz was playing over the store's speakers when Tariq arrived. Jamal was behind the counter, rattling the glass

73

countertop with a single drumstick. No-one else was in the store.

When he saw Tariq, he lowered the volume. 'If it ain't the liquorice stick man,' he said.

Everything this guy said was in code. Seeing Tariq's blank face, he added, 'Clarinet, man. Liquorice stick. Axe of choice for cats like Sidney Bechet and Harry Carney.'

Tariq searched for a way into the conversation. 'I like Richard Stoltzman,' he said.

Sticking out his lower lip, Jamal nodded. 'Rings a bell.'

'I think he plays jazz. Sometimes.'

'Maybe so. But we got to get you into the *real* shit.'

The first time Tariq visited the store, he'd been intimidated by its darkness and noise and Jamal's fierce intensity. But today it was an Aladdin's cave of music and coloured light, Jamal a genie with thousands of treasures at his disposal. He selected a record from a giant stack behind the counter and put it on the turntable. Reed section, piano, bass and drums. Music with a good-time Mardi Gras feel but also a weird, voodoo vibe.

'I like this,' Tariq said.

'Of course you do.'

It was marching music for ghosts. African Halloween. The block of reeds went quiet and the piano tinkled and a solo clarinet took off, dipping and weaving like a charmed cobra. The album cover, which Jamal set before Tariq, featured a man in sunglasses and battered stovepipe hat playing two saxophones at the same time.

'Rahsaan,' Jamal said, tapping the cover. 'The medicine man.'

'What's the point of that?' Tariq said, indicating the doubled saxophones.

Jamal nodded at the speaker. His goatee trembled. '*That's* the point.'

The music swirled. It tumbled and rolled. The clarinet gave way to a saxophone. Tariq found himself holding his breath. 'What is he *doing?*'

Jamal grinned and his gold tooth gleamed. 'Circular breathing.'

'I've heard of that.'

'Don't get *that* shit playing classical.'

Jamal was not wearing his African robe but an ensemble no less colourful: skullcap, collarless linen shirt, embroidered cotton jacket. His earring sparkled. The unused jacket sleeve had been folded and pinned to the shoulder.

'Name's Jamal, by the way.'

'I know.'

'Oh, yeah?'

'Someone told me.'

'What else they tell you?'

'Nothing.'

'I do carry a reputation.'

They listened to one record after another, interrupted on occasion by a customer. Every tune was strangely compelling. Furious rhythms. Bizarre melodies or no melodies at all. Squeaks and honks and prayerful shouts.

'It's like *choubi*,' Tariq said at one point.

'Say what?'

'Traditional Iraqi music. Or one tradition, anyway. My uncle transcribes it.'

'You'll play it for me.'

'I don't know about that.'

'Sure. On your liquorice stick. Next time.'

After an hour, Jamal spun a vinyl version of 'Impressions' so that Tariq could 'hear it like it was meant to be heard'. It was louder and even more stirring than Tariq's first listen on the radio, its dark tones and wrenching turns enhanced by the store's low ceilings and incense smells and Jamal's shaking head and snapping fingers. When it was over, Jamal slipped the ordered CD into a bag along with another Coltrane recording, 'My Favourite Things'.

'I only brought ten dollars,' Tariq said.

'And you get two bucks in change. Other disc is on the house. Can't be going home with only one Trane record. All part of your education. You listen to those for a while and then I'll turn you on to the spiritual stuff. *Ascension*, *A Love Supreme*. Pay your dues and get your reward.'

He took a deep breath, nostrils flaring. 'Coffee time!'

He locked up the store and put up a BACK IN TEN MINUTES sign and he and Tariq walked along the busy street.

'You drink coffee?' he asked.

'No.'

'Thought you said you was from Iraq.'

'I don't like it. Don't like tea either.'

'OK. Have a Coke. On me.'

They passed Starbucks ('corporate jive,' Jamal said with a sneer) and went into a coffee shop beside the music store. A skinny guy with dreadlocks, wearing a striped apron and a knitted Jamaican hat, came out from behind the counter. He and Jamal went through a complicated ritual of embrace, handshake and traded laughter.

'Say hello to Russell,' Jamal said. 'Best trumpet player out of the state of Florida since Fats Navarro.'

'Don't be listening to him, young man. He is a gentleman of exquisite prejudice and unreasonable loyalty.'

'Giving the kid a musical education.'

'No doubt.'

The men gabbed about music. Their talk was loose and rhythmic, like a piece of jazz itself, anchored by Jamal's tom-tom laugh and hissing hi-hat slang. Other customers came in, and Jamal and Tariq retreated to a table in the corner. Jamal stuck his long legs into the aisle. He wore baggy silk pants and sandals. His feet were huge.

'You in school, right?'

'Monroe High,' Tariq said.

'And today is ... what, exactly? Day off?'

When Tariq hesitated, Jamal added, 'Speaking of education.'

'I haven't been feeling too well lately.'

Jamal leaned back in the chair, sized him up. 'What about your folks?'

'They're at work.'

'They church people?'

'We don't call it church.'

'I know that. You do the whole *kuttab* thing?'

Tariq tensed with surprise. So far, this excursion into Jamal's world had been an escape from everything familiar. 'I studied when I was little,' he said carefully. 'At the Masjid As-Sunnah mosque.'

'On Lilac Street?'

'Yes.'

'You still go?'

'When they make me.'

'Which is ... ?'

'Pretty much all the time.'

Russell placed an espresso and a soda on their table and returned to his other customers. Jamal ripped open a sachet of sugar with his teeth, emptied it into the tiny cup and stirred slowly.

'I hear you,' he said. 'My daddy was a member of the Nation of Islam. You know about them, right?'

'I guess.'

'He was a "righteous teacher". Follower of Elijah Muhammad. Did social work with kids in Detroit, inner city, where he met my mama. I went to a Muhammad school, studied the Qur'an, the whole charade. No disrespect.' His voice was soft. The look on his face had changed. Still intense, but with a compressed seriousness. 'But I wanted to play basketball and listen to hip-hop and smoke weed. And girls, sure enough. Mosque ain't no place to meet the ladies, am I right?'

Tariq smiled and lowered his eyes.

'And I dug jazz,' Jamal said, 'even back then I dug it. The *original* hip-hop. I wanted the world, man, you know what I'm saying? I wanted the *groove*. So I took off. Circled the country. Went to Philadelphia and then Oakland and Denver and Texas. Worked as a longshoreman for a while in Galveston. Tracked back to Philly, got married, had a baby girl, picked up some bad habits. Come the millennium I was twenty-three years old and didn't have jack to show for it. Divorced and homeless and down on myself. So I do what the man tell you to do. Join the army. "Be all you can be" and all *that* bullshit.'

His face had hardened, the scar on his neck glowed and his eyes had a distant, crystalline bitterness.

'Is that how you lost your arm?' Tariq said.

Jamal looked at the pinned jacket sleeve. His face twitched, as if touched by an electric wire. When he spoke, his tone was flat, his voice hollow. 'I don't talk about that.'

'OK.'

Tariq sipped his soda. Something easeful had been squeezed from the air. Jamal's head was perfectly still, but energy radiated from him like heat off the desert. He stared over Tariq's shoulder intently, drum-rolling the tabletop with his fingertips.

He blinked dramatically and pulled at his nose. 'You and your family,' he said. 'When y'all move to the States?'

'When I was four.'

'Before the invasion?'

'Mm.'

'And what part of Baghdad did you live in?'

'Al-Jadriya.'

Jamal grimaced. He finished the dregs of his coffee and ran a palm over his head, as if smoothing a mass of imaginary hair. 'So. Young man. I want you listen to Trane till you can hum his solos. Note for note. Think you can do that?'

'I can try.'

Jamal fished change from his pockets, counted it out and left it on the table. As they left the coffee shop he pointed at Russell, who grinned from behind the counter and winked at Tariq.

Outside, Jamal stood tall in the afternoon light, as distinguished as an African chief. With its force and colour, his figure was like a maypole in the busy street, and the solid world of ivy-clad buildings and old streetlamps and towering trees seemed to revolve and blur around him. Tariq looked at him with awe. For once he had found someone he could talk to, someone with the authority of experience who would listen to him about the terror of school, the distance of Rachel, the suffocating attention of his parents. Someone who would respond not with rote commands but understanding and encouragement.

'Don't tell me,' Jamal said. 'You heading home to rest and recuperate. Seeing how you ain't feeling so hot.'

'To practise.'

'No medicine like music, my friend. And when you –'

Jamal's face froze mid-sentence. His forehead crinkled; his lip lifted in a nasty curl. 'Look what we got here,' he said, staring up the street.

'What?'

'They come sniffing round here last spring,' he said in a

steely voice. 'Twice a week. College back in session and they back too, flapping like buzzards.'

Two military men in dress uniform came into view, walking towards them. One tall and thin, a black guy, with a pencil moustache and some swagger in his step; and a heavy-set white guy with a dull oval face and small eyes. They laughed and joked, but when they saw Jamal they went quiet. Jamal stepped in front of them so they had to stop.

'Hello, Jamal,' the black guy said. 'You cool today?'

'Cool every day, Rafer. How 'bout you?'

Rafer removed his hat, revealing eyes that were steady and alert. 'Just doing my job.'

'That right? Telling lies? Breaking promises? You go to the VA Hospital like I told you?'

'What say you let us be on our way, Jamal,' Rafer said. 'Nobody wants a scene.'

Jamal shifted from foot to foot, rolling his shoulders and bobbing his head like a boxer readying himself for a fight. 'A scene? That what you call it? A man tells it like he sees it, exercises his constitutional right to call out a pile of shit when it laying there on the sidewalk, and you make it sound like some kind of down-home *craziness*?'

Rafer glanced at Tariq. 'What we would like, Jamal, is to be allowed to exercise *our* right to speak to young people about their future. How they can be the best with us. How they can realise their potential and help their country at the same time.'

Tariq knew that the officer was speaking that way for his benefit; he had that phony teacher tone. The other guy was listening carefully, his small eyes flicking back and forth from Rafer to Jamal. A breeze stirred the trees above them, and something in its feel called forth a distant memory for Tariq: a desert chill invading the humidity and leafiness of fading summer.

Jamal erupted. 'Bull*shit*!' he shouted. 'You telling them it's all a computer game. Or a fucking music video. Lace up your boots, soldier, we playing Call of Duty. Like sitting on the couch and punching buttons and splattering cartoon characters. Get your iTunes cranked up and your headphones on and go on out and *waste* the enemy. Who you think you fooling? *I* was that kid, Rafer.'

Jamal was in a frenzy, his arm flailing and his head thrusting like a turkey's. Flecks of spittle had collected at the corners of his mouth and a bead of sweat tracked down his temple. Rafer's partner had backed away, one boot off the sidewalk. Passersby watched and listened.

'You like doing the devil's work, Rafer? You like rounding up souls so they can ride off to hell? Wasting kids like Tariq here when they're not getting blown away themselves? This is why I ain't paid a nickel in taxes these last four years. I ain't financing evil. *Oh*, no.'

'Whatever we're doing,' Rafer said softly, 'it isn't evil, Jamal.'

Jamal wiped his mouth and took a deep breath. Rafer met his gaze full on. But when Jamal raised his hand and bared his teeth as if to continue the rant, he suddenly went limp, like a burst balloon. He covered his eyes with his hand, made a sound like a wounded animal and, pushing Rafer aside, ran up the street.

The quiet officer whistled between his teeth. Rafer had his hat tucked between ribs and elbow, like a man with bad news. He looked at Tariq with curiosity, as if sizing up the dark hair and Semitic features, wondering where he was from.

Then, as the breeze puffed a bit of grit into Tariq's eye, the geometry of this scene – a public place, soldiers tense and watchful, a boy witnessing confrontation – suggested a different landscape, where dust filled the streets and the sound of gunfire was as regular as the call to prayer. The scent of fear was in the air. Beyond, Jamal strode away, not back to the store but out along the millrace. As his bald head and lanky form receded, weaving unsteadily, Tariq felt naked and exposed, and the despair of recent weeks, which had disappeared over the two hours he had been with Jamal, swallowed him like a snake.

Chapter 9

THE SOCCER MATCH against the Az-Zahra Madressah was scheduled for nine o'clock on Saturday so that it would be finished before midday prayer. Tariq had not spoken to his father all week. He told his mother that, after his spells of illness, he was too weak to play. Malik insisted he at least be available as a sub. Then early that morning Mumtaz Abdul phoned the imam to say that he and his brother could not make the match. The mosque team was down to eleven men, with no substitutes. Tariq was forced to commit to ninety minutes.

He cycled to the mosque so that he would not have to be alone with his father and sat at the opposite end of the basement room where they changed into their uniforms. Tariq's hands shook as he tied his boots. The madressah players dressed across the hall, and their laughter and loud African voices made him nervous. He had seen them arrive: a sprinkling of Iranians but mostly Nigerians and Ugandans, big and boisterous, with eyes as fierce and focused as Jamal's. Imam Mohammad, who had agreed to referee the match along with the madressah imam, shuttled between the locker rooms, making arrangements and announcing every few minutes that the match was an exercise in Islamic unity. He looked bizarre in his black referee's outfit.

All of Tariq's team-mates were from the Middle East. Some, like Mahmoud Khan and his son Mohammad, were friends of the family, fellow-Iraqis who lived an hour north of Monroe.

Others were men in their late twenties and thirties, professionals and postgraduate students. Tariq's father was one of the oldest, but as he had played semi-professionally in Iraq he had been selected captain.

Mohammad Khan was the only player close in age to Tariq. Soft-spoken and shy, he had graduated from Monroe High last year and now studied full-time at an Islamic centre in Milwaukee. It was said that he wanted to become an imam and return to Iraq. The other young men Tariq did not know well. They were confident and worldly, and strutted around the locker room with their shirts off, ribbing each other and ignoring the young guys and their ancient fathers.

"'A group of Arabs did it",' Sahar Nassam said. 'I was walking through the lunchroom when I heard it. Or maybe it was "a *bunch* of Arabs".'

Sahar stood in the middle of the room, wearing only boxer shorts. His beard was closely trimmed, his torso hairless and muscular. Easy in his near nakedness, he stood on the balls of his feet, taking off jewellery piece by piece: gold necklace and bracelet, signet ring, heavy gold watch. He was a clinical analyst at a pharmaceutical company in Kenosha, on an executive track, he liked to say. The words he quoted were from a conversation he had overheard at his workplace during the week.

'A bunch of Arabs did what?' Abdel Taman asked.

'What do you think? 9/11. And he says it just when I'm passing their table.'

This detail sharpened the room's atmosphere, like a strange sound in the middle of the night.

'What do you expect?' Abdel said. 'Now that Bin Laden's dead, it's on everybody's lips again.'

Malik made a face, as if he'd eaten something rancid.

'They can *talk* about it,' Sahar said. 'I have no objection. It's what he was saying to me. About *us*.'

'He could have said worse,' Mahmoud said.

'He did. Or *someone* did. I was leaving the room and a different voice said, "I still don't trust any of them." Loud enough to make sure I heard. A Jewish voice.'

Mahmoud, who had his foot on the bench to tie his bootlaces, shrugged and yanked at the lace ends. 'So he doesn't trust you. Do you trust him?'

'Whether I do or not, I'm not going to insult him in his presence. Or his race.'

'Arabs are not a race,' Abdel said.

'What do you mean?' Sahar said.

Sahar seemed to make a big show of being assimilated. A real American. He would have fit right in in the showers after gym class. If the older men hadn't been there, Tariq was sure, Sahar and Abdel would have been talking about the women they had pulled in the nightclubs out on Route 54.

Abdel pulled his singlet over his head and smoothed the satin fabric against his chest. He was a lawyer with his own practice on Gate Street. 'If anything, we are an ethnic group,' he said.

'Same thing,' Sahar said.

'No, it's not.'

Mahmoud let his boot hit the tiled floor with a clatter and stretched to full height. He was a tall man with a huge stomach and heavy shoulders.

'You two, stop talking nonsense,' he said.

He spoke in Arabic, and the change of language was like a shift in the weather. He glanced at Malik.

Sahar ignored him. 'You're from Cairo,' he said to Abdel.

'That's right.'

'Egyptians always think they know more about being an Arab than anyone else.'

Abdel laughed. 'Well, of course. Do I have to give you a history lesson?'

Malik stepped forward. He was agitated. 'You heard Mahmoud,' he said sharply. 'This is no way to be talking in a mosque.'

Sahar made a show of looking around the room. 'Mosque? This is a basement, Malik.'

'We are on sacred ground.'

'So – we can't mention 9/11? Or what it means to be an Arab? Is that what you're saying? What are you worried about? Let's get the imam in here, see what he has to say on the subject.'

'We have a match to play,' Malik said testily. 'You should be getting ready for competition. Do you want to lose to *them*?'

He pointed in the direction of the opposition. As if on cue, a volley of laughter sounded from across the hall.

'Oh, they sound *really* focused,' Sahar said. 'Lighten up, Malik, and worry about your own game. I don't plan on losing to anyone.'

'Don't speak to the captain like that,' Mahmoud shouted. 'Show some respect.'

Abdel and Sahar exchanged glances. Associated with the old men, Tariq shrank in embarrassment. The room stayed silent until the team was ready to take to the field.

On the pitch, Tariq felt small and cold. Low in the sky was a bank of cloud as heavy as a wet towel. Thin rain, and a cutting wind from the north. The mosque team warmed up, listlessly passing the ball in a team circle. The locker room spat had drained their spirit. The madressah team ran on to the field as if released from prison. Leaping and yelling and slapping each other enthusiastically. Most of them were massive. Great hands and broad shoulders. Round, sub-Saharan faces. A flash of teeth and eyes. They seemed about to burst out of their uniforms, and the sound when they kicked the ball was like a boxer slamming a punch-bag.

Malik put Tariq at left back, beside Sahar. The position, he knew, had nothing to do with quickness or ability to defend; it was simply the spot on the pitch where he would do the least damage. Yet he was scared of letting down the side. And, sure enough, as soon as the match began he was out of his depth. The madressah strikers were fast and aggressive, if not hugely skilled. They barrelled over Mohammad and Adbel and the other mid-fielders. Only Sahar could stay with them, and he had no support. Within ten minutes their centre, a tall Ugandan with thighs like lamp-posts, elbowed Sahar to the ground and rifled a shot past Mahmoud in goals. After scoring he lifted his shirt above his head and leapt about with ungracious enthusiasm. Malik complained to the imams. The goal stood.

'Where were *you*?' Malik shouted at Tariq, his face dark with anger. He was red-faced and winded.

'Leave the kid alone,' Sahar said.

'Mind your own business.' Malik bared his teeth and thrust his face close to Sahar's. 'One of you is no better than the other,' he said.

The game proceeded. Tariq felt as if surrounded by hungry dogs. Early in the second half, with the mosque team down 2-0, one of the Nigerians took a high cross off his chest, swivelled, and back-heeled the ball into the box. Lunging to intercept, Sahar took himself out of the play. Only Tariq stood between the madressah player and Mahmoud in goals. Back-pedalling, he tracked the ball as best he could, but the big striker thrust out a forearm and knocked him easily to the turf. With only the keeper to beat, he measured carefully and chipped an easy goal into the corner of the net.

More celebrations. More complaints to the refs. The wind knocked out of him, Tariq slowly picked himself up and bent over, hands on his knees. Malik sprinted across the pitch, fists clenched. Tariq thought he was headed for the ref, but suddenly his face was inches from Tariq's.

'You call that defending? You are useless. Do you hear me? Get off the pitch. I don't know why I asked you. We'd be better off if you *weren't here.*'

Rage churned in Tariq's throat and his vision grew blurred. Without conscious intent, he leapt on his father, shouting and clawing and choking with tears. They fell to the ground. As they rolled around, he hit Malik on the side of the head as hard as he could. Mahmoud and several of the young men pulled the two of them apart. Tariq could see nothing but the ragged edges of ground and sky and heard only his own bellowing sobs. The rain had thickened and his uniform was covered in mud. When he rose at last, Imam Mohammad had taken firm hold of his elbow. He escorted Tariq off the pitch and told him to go to the locker room.

HE sat before his locker in his stocking feet, his boots upturned on the tiles, his knees shaking. Dried mud in the corners, smells of wintergreen and stale sweat, watery light barely penetrating the smoked glass panes above the lockers. Down to ten men, the mosque team played on. The sounds of the game echoed in the empty space and the wind and rain swept across the roof like the lash of a whip.

He was far away from anything that might give him comfort. He rubbed his damp skin, which barely held in the turmoil of his blood.

Imam Mohammad came in, water dripping from his beard, his dark hair slick as a seal's.

'A tempest out there,' he said. 'And it wasn't forecast.'

'Is the match over?' Tariq said.

He shook his head. 'Ten minutes left. Five-nil. Imam Hamid can finish on his own.'

He turned on the overhead light and took a towel from his locker. He took off his jersey, dried his beard and vigorously rubbed his hair. Tariq pushed at his muddy boots with his toe. The imam sat beside him. Without his robe and turban, his chest hair matted to his drooping chest, he looked not like a religious leader but an ordinary man, old and wrinkled and faintly comical.

'Are you all right?'

'I don't know.'

'Your father told me you've been ill.'

'Is that what he said?'

'You disagree?'

'No. It's true.'

'Somehow I suspect it's not physical.'

Tariq shrugged.

'It's not easy, is it?' the imam said.

Searching for a phrase that would put off the inevitable lecture, Tariq was overcome by a rush of self-pity. It was like the moments deep at night when he lay awake in despair, without light, without company, without music. When the burden of his existence lay on him like a pile of dirt. It seemed at such times that he was face to face with his essential self. Family, religion, school, friends – what were they, anyway, but circumstances that had been heaped on top of who he was? Strip them away and what was left? What clues remained as to why he existed at all?

'Do you ever wonder what's the point?' Tariq said. 'I mean, the point of going on?'

He was crying again. The imam laid the damp towel across his lap and waited for Tariq to gather himself. 'Of course,' he said. 'I wonder about that every day. We must all wonder. It is part of being a good Muslim.'

'No, I mean the point of doing *anything*. At *all*.'

Tariq was louder than he intended, and his voice echoed in the bleak room. The imam laid a hand on his shoulder. '*Whenever you see someone better than you in wealth, face or figure, you should look at someone who is inferior to you in these respects.* So the prophet said. We must remember how lucky we are, Tariq. How much we have that most of our brothers do not.'

'It's not a question of what I have or don't have. That doesn't have anything to do with it. I don't have *control*. Over my own life.'

'Who does? Allah controls all, every schoolboy knows that. Turn to Allah in all situations. Remember his names. "I place my trust in Allah, and there is no power except with Allah."'

His voice was as steady as the wind and rain. But what had Tariq expected him to say? He was an imam. Respect your father. Turn to Allah. All will be well.

Baba. Allah. Father knows best.

'I don't see how Allah has anything to do with it,' Tariq said bitterly. 'We are always being told to think of the life beyond. To live for what is to come. But what about *this* life, the here and now. That's what's so hard.'

Tariq expected an angry response, but the imam spoke softly. 'You might be surprised to hear this, but I have felt the same things. Many times. Especially when I was a young man. But you know what I have learned? That Allah's power is mighty because he can choose not to use it. He knows when not to punish.

He knows when to forgive. And forgiveness brings light to all the dark places that sit inside of us.'

'Nobody forgives me when *I* mess up.'

'Allah does. "All praise and gratitude for God." Repeat that whenever you feel lost. It will help. I promise.'

He patted Tariq's shoulder and resumed towelling his wet hair. Outside, the ref's whistle shrieked beneath the lash of the rain.

Chapter 10

TARIQ was doing a pop quiz in math class when the teacher slid a note onto the corner of his desk. It was a request from the school counsellor to see him at 11:30, when he had a free period.

Ms Wessell's office was tucked away at the end of the administration hall, out of main sightlines so that students could come and go discreetly. The furniture was comfortable and contemporary, free soda was on hand, and the walls were hung with reprints of famous works of Impressionism and a motivational poster with the word AMBITION beneath a photograph of a woman at the peak of a snowy mountain.

As soon as he was seated, Ms Wessell said, 'How's class been going, Tariq?' She pronounced his name as if it rhymed with Derek. 'Mr Broquist is doing *Rhapsody in Blue* for the holiday gala, isn't that right? What a *wonderful* opportunity for a clarinet player.'

Tariq nodded sullenly. He hated how adults in school started awkward conversations by pretending they were interested in *you*. Dropping personal detail into small talk. Mentioning how they loved something you happened to be involved in. The next thing she'd be telling him how terrifically *diverse* the band was, with such an *interesting* Middle Eastern strain. At least the imam gave you the Islamic line straight up, no bullshit.

'Last year was *so* uplifting,' she said. 'The march by Prokofiev, such a lively piece, and since we really can't do religious music … well, it was very moving.'

'Did you make me come here to talk about music?' Tariq said.

Ms Wessell smiled at him steadily. She had a small face, short grey hair, cut stylishly, and pearl earrings shaped like teardrops, which trembled softly as she considered her reply.

'I don't *make* anyone do anything, Tariq. I've asked you here because I think it might be in your interest to talk to me. Because my role here, as you know, is to help, to be *of* help, especially when students have challenges that might be hard to talk about elsewhere.'

She tilted her head and smiled.

He knew the game. He was supposed to open up, to show in a roundabout way that he knew why he was here and so benefit all the more from the school's caring philosophy, which, in case there was any doubt about its articulation, was emblazoned in red felt letters on a wall-hanging behind Ms Wessell's desk: EVERY STUDENT IS SPECIAL.

But he said nothing.

Still smiling, she tapped her desktop with a pen and lifted a piece of paper. 'I got a note from Mr Corboy. You've had seven full-day absences since school began.'

'We had our holiday at the end of Ramadan. I was excused.'

'He didn't count the holiday period.'

'I've been sick.'

She glanced at the paper. *Still* smiling. 'School's only been in session for twenty days, Tariq. Keep going at this rate and you'll fall short of the annual state requirement before Christmas.' She cleared her throat. 'I mean the holidays.'

'I can't help it if I'm sick.'

She laid the paper aside and spoke with throaty intimacy. 'I telephoned your house. Two or three times. No answer. Spoke to your teachers. You know the school policy. Now, I've held off sending a letter to your parents until we could meet, you and I.'

'A letter?'

She had his attention. Swivelling her leather chair to her computer, she put on her reading glasses and peered at the screen. 'You saw the nurse. No physical problems that she could assess … possibility of some emotional dissonance.'

'What's that supposed to mean?'

She removed her glasses. 'Is there anything that's upset you recently? School-related, home-related? You know that anything you say in here is in complete confidence.'

He shook his head.

'The nurse noticed *something*,' she continued. 'Your teachers too.'

'I haven't been feeling well. I had to fast for a whole month, I couldn't have breakfast or lunch, you have no idea, your whole routine gets turned upside down.'

Her lips were pressed together, her eyes were alert. Perched on the edge of her soft chair, pen raised like a magic wand, she was ready to solve all his problems. 'I'm glad you brought that up,' she said. 'I have a question for you: is it possible that you underestimate the challenges associated with your ethnicity. And your religious persuasion?'

'What do you mean?'

'Well, that others in the school may see you in a way that disempowers you. Boys especially, with not that much experience of diversity, they can buy in to certain stereotypes about Arab-Americans.'

'I'm Iraqi.'

She raised her chin and crinkled her eyes like a gambler holding a winning card. 'And if that perception, let's say, leads to a type of physical intimidation – you know, what used to be called hazing – well, such an incident, were it to happen, might be hard for someone like you to escalate to the right people.'

94

Inflated by her rhetoric, she seemed to float above the chair, her shoulders lifted, the spikes of her hair quivering. The jargon baffled him. He spread his hands wearily – and then her meaning hit him like a truck.

She knew about Brad. Someone had told her. A cold wave of fear rippled through his chest.

'I don't know what you're talking about,' he said.

She nodded quickly. 'Your impulse will be to deny. Of course. But the people who witnessed the incident are concerned about you, Tariq. The *school* is concerned. And there is nothing to be afraid of. The situation is clear. You know the zero tolerances here. Drugs. Bullying.'

'Drugs?'

'And bullying. There are those who witnessed. And will back you up. But you have to bring the case.'

Outside the office, fluttering against the window like the wings of birds, were the stiff branches of the juniper bush that screened Ms Wessell's talks from anyone who might be walking past. Tariq folded his hands and pressed them between his knees. 'You make it sound like a court of law.'

'That's not a bad analogy. Do your parents know?'

'Know what?'

'About the incident.'

The contours of the room blurred, and little darts of anxiety flitted at the edges of his vision like shooting stars. She had ambushed him. Just like Brad in the parking lot, she had jumped him when he least expected it.

He stood up. 'I have to go.'

'Now, Tariq.'

'Nothing happened,' he said.

'Excuse me?'

'Or if anything did, it was just horsing around. It's all a misunderstanding. Whoever told you about it should mind their own business.'

ON the surface, nothing in his routine was different over the rest of that day – he sat in class, visited his locker, practised his clarinet – but Tariq recognised none of it. His old existence had vanished. Between bells, he pushed his way through the crowded hallways clutching his books, staring straight ahead. It was as if every word was about him, as if every glance came his way. The polished floors, the fluorescent gleam of the classrooms, the long rows of lockers with their vented doors and combination knobs – the school had become a shell of artificial surfaces and alien objects. Like a movie set. Nothing felt real except the cold certainty that he was in more danger than ever.

At any moment he expected Brad to appear with vengeance on his breath. He must know the word was out. He must believe that Tariq had squealed. And though he made it through the day and out of the grounds without meeting Brad, Tariq imagined him like a villain in a play, biding his time in the wings, sharpening his sword.

He expected to find relief at home, but that night, when his parents were in bed and the utter silence was broken only by the occasional swish of late traffic, he felt the contours of his life melt in the dark. His very existence seeped into the gloom, out of his control, a puddle of loose terror. He felt like a character in one of Uncle Rahim's traditional songs: caught in a cycle of suffering that promised no end. Why couldn't he sleep? Before, the stress had come and gone. Now, it burned incessantly.

At the deepest point of the night he rose from his bed and looked out the window. Pale moonlight fell between the houses, turning violet the packed earth of the Greenbriars' side yard. Electricity wires sliced through the gloom and shadows stretched along the street. A basement window glowed. If only darkness and its escape might last forever. As Hamlet wished.

A sudden movement startled him, and a cat padded across the vista with a dead bird in its mouth.

WHEN he opened his locker next morning, a note fell out. It was crudely written in pencil:

> Hey freak show, youre not the only people who can
> terrorise. Keep your mouth shut if you dont want to get
> fucked up big time.

As he read these words, his locker door rattled. Dazed, he slid the note into his pocket.

It was Rachel. She made a show of acting goofy and distracted, but her eyes were watchful. As she leaned in to his shoulder, her breast grazed his arm, but he was too numb to be excited by the contact.

'Hey, stranger,' she said.

'Hi.'

'You're white as a ghost. You feeling OK?'

'I keep getting this stomach thing.'

'Yeah?'

'Yeah.'

She wore frayed cut-offs and red tights with runs in both legs and black Converse shoes. A striped Van Heusen shirt with the cuffs folded over her forearms and the top three buttons undone.

'I lost five pounds,' she said.

'Really?'

She spread her arms. He blushed.

'It's the dancing. It's like working out. But I keep wondering: why are Middle Eastern dancers so fat?'

'That's not very nice.'

'No, it isn't, is it?'

He took his history book from his locker and closed the door. Between the note in his pocket and the smell of her funky perfume, he had grown dizzy. He steadied himself with a hand on the wall.

'You finish your history paper?' he said.

She squinted behind her glasses. 'I was on Facebook this morning,' she said. 'You closed your page.'

'Yeah.'

'You don't answer your phone. What's going on, Tariq?'

'Nothing.'

He walked away. She followed.

'Why are you avoiding me?'

'I'm not.'

'Is it because of the dancing? Some weird territorial thing, like you don't want me doing anything faintly Arabic?'

'That's ridiculous.'

'I know. But how else am I supposed to understand the way you're treating me?'

'It's hard to explain.'

She stopped, hands on hips, and snorted. '*Obviously*.'

'I'll see you in history class,' he said.

For the rest of the day, she didn't speak to him or look his way. He got in trouble several times for failing to pay attention in class. His stomach *did* hurt. School life flickered about him unnoticed. Scenarios and options seethed in his head.

After his final class he went up to the row of senior lockers on the second floor. He waited beside the water fountain until he saw Annalise arrive at her locker. He walked up to her.

'Hi, Annalise.'

'Sinbad,' she said, '*hi*. What brings you up to Mount Olympus?'

'I wanted to ask you something.'

'Rachel says you're Mr Freeze these days. She likes you. But why do I think you know that? You should know better than to play with a girl's affections.'

'I'm not playing anything.'

'No?'

Her wide mouth smiled suggestively. It was a cruel mouth, lips large and soft, blurred at the edges.

'Listen, I was wondering…' He dropped his voice. 'Can you buy me some weed?'

She pouted gleefully. 'Sinbad. I'm impressed. Took you for a normie.'

Her husky voice caressed him. She had allowed her top to slip over her shoulder, exposing her bra strap. Her hair was thick and mussed, the grain of her skin smooth. The blood jumped in his wrists and knees. But it had nothing to do with her come-on. She was no Rachel. It was the transaction he was suggesting.

'Don't call me Sinbad.'

'Maybe I should call you Stoner.'

'Look, can you get the stuff for me or not?'

She reached into her locker and rooted at the back and came up with a joint. Perfectly rolled, tapered, equipped with a cardboard filter. She touched his arm. 'Want a little taste now?' she said. 'Let's go out to the cottonwoods and light up.'

He took the joint from her. It was like holding the key to a secret door.

'I'll keep it for later,' he said.

'Suit yourself.'

'What do I owe you?'

She leaned close so that their shoulders bumped. 'My treat. Just don't be going off and doing anything crazy.'

He walked to the gas station and bought a lighter. He returned to the school and waited near the band room for half an hour. When he knew that Mr Kuntz was starting his rounds, he went into the boys' bathroom beside the cafeteria, closed the windows, lit up the joint and puffed for a minute or so. He didn't inhale. By the time Mr Kuntz arrived the air was blue with smoke.

'Tariq? Is that you?'

He walked across the tiles and handed Mr Kuntz the roach.

Chapter 11

IN THE PANIC that followed, Tariq was almost serene. He was safe, at least for now. The school's drug policy meant immediate, indefinite suspension. Mr Kuntz brought him to the discipline office, had him sign an admission of responsibility in the presence of the vice-principal, and summoned the nurse for a physical examination. The roach was sealed in a plastic bag and put in the school safe. The Monroe Police drug liaison, the vice-principal said gravely, would have to be contacted. Tariq's parents would be officially notified. Tariq was sent home and told not to return until the administration had decided how to handle his case.

He floated through these events in a bubble of relief. His fate was out of his hands.

Leaving the school grounds was like getting out of prison. The avenue that led away from the entrance was arched with elm trees, now losing their leaves, and Tariq walked with a light step past the funeral home, the old Masonic lodge, the dental clinic. High, thin cloud edged the sky and the air smelled like football and Halloween.

But the bubble burst when he reached home. His parents sat in the living room like figures in a mural. Malik held a prayer book in his hands. His jaw quivered.

'Tariq,' his mother said. 'What have you done?'

Her voice was thin and strange. She was dressed in a simple brown robe and grey hijab. The skin on her face was pale, soft and puffy, her eyes shiny.

'Did they call you?' Tariq said.

His father stood up, waving his arms. 'Of course they called us, what do you think? Called me at work, I was with a patient. Do you have any idea what it is like to get news like that in the middle of an ordinary day? It is like a gun going off.'

His father's words were clipped and guttural, as if they were making him gag. Tariq stared at the floor. The room's imported furnishings – the soft pillows and lacquered boxes and short-legged chairs – became part of the accusation. It was as if they were back in Baghdad, in crisis. He had shamed his family. His culture.

'Do you have anything to say for yourself?'

'It was only marijuana.'

'*Only*? So you are familiar with other drugs. You have experience?'

'Tariq,' Zaida said, 'what about cocaine? Crystal meth?' She turned to Malik. 'These are the big problem drugs at the university. Epidemic proportions, some are saying.'

'Is this why you attacked me during the football match?' Malik demanded. 'Were you high on drugs?'

'You attacked me first.' Tariq pointed towards the kitchen. 'In there.'

His father balled his hands into fists and looked at Zaida. 'This is what happens when discipline breaks down. When authority is questioned.'

'How long has this been going on?' Zaida said to Tariq.

'It hasn't been going on. It's just something I tried. And I don't do other drugs.'

'But you *do* marijuana,' his father said. 'Is it this jazz you're listening to?'

'Don't be ridiculous.'

'It's this Rachel girl. This Jew. Has she hooked you?'

'Malik,' Zaida said.

'I'm not hooked. It was the first time. Ever. And Rachel has nothing to do with it. All I did was smoke a little bit of weed.'

What trap had he set for himself? His parents had been transformed. Like a village woman adrift in the big city, his mother gazed about herself with puzzlement and fear. Malik paced the living room, his face mottled with rage. Tariq watched him warily. Zaida rose from her chair and went into the kitchen.

'Is this why we brought you to America and gave you a perfect life?' Malik shouted. 'So we could be humiliated?'

'My life? *Perfect?*'

Zaida made tea that none of them drank. Dinner was forgotten. Darkness fell and the house grew poisoned with bad feeling. His father swung between anger and blank distraction. His mother wept several times without warning. But Tariq stayed near her; Malik would not hit him with her so close. Or would he?

They insisted that Tariq attend mosque that evening. Afterwards the imam took him alone to an inner room, lined with rugs and prayer mats, and spoke at length, building on his sermon in the locker room. He recommended fasting. He assured Tariq that the dangers of alcohol were equally present in hashish. He recited from the Qur'an: *Satan's plan is to sow hatred and enmity amongst you with intoxicants and gambling, and to hamper you from the remembrance of Allah and from prayer.* He reviewed the twenty different ways that intoxicants were 'the mother of all evils'. Tariq nodded and agreed at the right moments. He promised never again to commit such a sin. He did whatever was required for the painful session to end.

The school had imposed a so-called cooling-off period of two days, after which his parents would meet the principal. In the meantime he was grounded. Zaida cancelled her classes, but after a morning of aimless interrogation and occasional harangue, she returned to college. Relieved to be at last free of scrutiny, Tariq lay in his bed, listening to the radio and playing along with his clarinet. Though he left his phone off, occasionally he checked for messages. Rachel had returned to his thoughts. Perversely, his father's suspicion of her had pleased him. In the coldness of his predicament, she was a warm spot of desire, though he was as distant as ever from being able to tell her. She did not call or leave any messages.

His parents returned from the school meeting more shaken than ever. Another council in the living room. They asked him bluntly: was he being bullied?

'Who told you that?'

'Mr Moscowitz,' Zaida said. 'He said they have reason to believe that you have been harassed. That perhaps the incident in the bathroom was because of that.'

The hope in his mother's eyes was frail.

'That's stupid. Why would I do that?'

'What about this fight in the parking lot?' Malik said. His suit was rumpled and his hair unkempt, as if he had slept in his clothes. He leaned forward, elbows on his knees. Tariq could see the conflict in his face: afraid it might be true; half hoping it would be, if only to get his son off the hook of the suspension.

'There was no fight.'

'That's not what Mr Moscowitz said.'

'Was he there?'

'Have you learned nothing I've taught you? You see trouble, you steer clear.'

'Look, what happened, happened. I did the crime, I'll do the time.'

Enraged at Tariq's tone, his father moved to strike him. Zaida stepped between them.

'*Habibi*,' she said to Tariq, 'Mr Moscowitz is understanding. He said that if the school thought you were under pressure from others they would treat you more leniently.'

'He did not say that,' Malik shouted. 'You never get anything right. You, with all your grand education.'

'Malik, go into the kitchen. Now. Give me a minute with him.'

Malik left the room, bobbing like a puppet. Satisfaction at his father's loss of control spread through Tariq's veins like a drug.

'First your behaviour at the soccer game,' Zaida said quietly, 'now this. It's no wonder your father is at the end of his patience.'

Tariq smirked. 'He's always at the end of his patience.'

She started to speak, then held back. The planes of her face were creased, her fingers knit with worry. He knew the words that would lift her pain, but he didn't say them.

THEY left him alone for a day and then sent in Rahim. He arrived the next afternoon, limping, carrying his oud. Tariq was alone in the house.

'Rickey, how are you? I have a new song for you.'

Tariq put on the kettle and prepared the teacups while Rahim washed and changed from work overalls into the loose robe he liked to wear when playing. Tariq heard him coughing in the bathroom. The true reason for his presence was like white noise. But when he returned to the living room he said nothing. He picked up his instrument and played.

It was not *choubi* but a song made popular by Gabriel Malek, a love song in a strange tuning. Rahim's singing voice was rough at the edges and breathy at times, but full of passion. The instrumental break was his own arrangement.

'It's beautiful,' Tariq said when he was finished. 'But not Arabic.'

'No. Aramaic. Malek was Assyrian.'

He played several more songs. He produced music from his satchel, with another new arrangement for oud and clarinet. They practised for a while, and tension was lost in the chords and intervals.

'Can I play you something?' Tariq said.

'Of course.'

He had abandoned the Gershwin. He wouldn't be playing in the Thanksgiving concert. He moistened the reed and set his fingers. Hesitantly, he played the opening bars of 'In a Sentimental Mood'. He had found the score online.

'That's all I know. So far.'

'Duke Ellington.'

'You know it?'

'Every musician knows Ellington. Or should.'

'What do you think?'

Rahim winked. 'Keep practising.'

Afterwards they sat in the kitchen drinking tea. The oud was propped against the refrigerator. Rahim had brought pastries from the Lebanese bakery and a jar of pickled peaches.

'Ellington came to Baghdad,' Rahim said as they ate. 'In 1963. Your grandfather was very excited, bought tickets for the whole family. The adults, anyhow. I was five years old. But I remember that the night before the public concert his band played for the US embassy in the al-Khuld Hall. It was on television, and we watched at my uncle's restaurant. The next day there was a coup and the concert was cancelled. My father talked about it for years. The Ba'ath party ruined *his* party, he used to say.'

'So Iraqis like jazz.'

'Well. It was the pop music of my father's generation. But it's not *maqam*, Rickey.'

He wiped his fingers with a napkin and picked up his oud.

'Those Malek songs,' Rahim said, '*that's* what you should learn. He may have been a Christian, but he was the best.' He played some chords. 'Years ago I met him. Before he left for Beirut. The finest oud player I ever heard. He could play anything. Master of *maqam*, of course, but he would play flamenco in his solos, or Indian music. He knew exactly what to do. It always worked.'

As he spoke he softly played examples.

'He was a gentleman. And intelligent. Made sure he got his family out before it was too late. Though not all of them followed his lead. When I ended up in al-Jadriya, I found out that his cousin was there. Someone like me, not enough brains to leave when he had the chance. Two of the guards were Kurdish. If you think Shias can hate, you should have seen how those Kurds treated him.'

He put the oud on the floor. As always when he talked about his time in prison, his face went stiff.

'His cell was next to mine. He screamed when they took him out and moaned when they brought him back.'

'Why was he there?'

'Because he was Assyrian. Me, they thought I knew something about al-Kamara, the parliamentary leader who went missing. My torturers were sadists, but logical sadists. Malek's cousin ... they were hurting him for pleasure. Beating him with cables, hanging him from the ceiling by his feet, plastic sticks up his anus.'

'Ammu Rahim. Please.'

'You know what? He was *nice* to them. Tried to bribe them. Pretended that it was all a mistake. That if he ignored them they would go away.'

'Do we have to talk about this?'

Tariq rose from his seat and collected the dirty cups and saucers. They rattled as he carried them to the sink. He wet a dishcloth and wiped the counter clean. Pale sunlight slanted through the venetian blinds and striped the floor.

'I hear you met the imam,' Rahim said.

'Twice.'

'So you're rising in the world.'

'Am I?'

Rahim smiled. 'Imam Mohammad's advice is very valuable. Just do the opposite of what he tells you and you can't go wrong.'

'I'll try to remember that.'

Tariq leaned against the counter. Rahim stared at the tabletop, frowning. His arms lay folded tightly against his large stomach. He looked wistfully at the oud, as if to say, *the time for music is over*.

'Rickey. There comes a point when it's no use to run.'

'I'm not running.'

'If you can't get back into Monroe High, you'll be sent to the mosque school. You'll end up listening to the imam all day. Is that what you want?'

'I don't know what I want.'

Rahim stood up. Lifted his shoulders. His face was dark, and the pink scars on his neck glowed like stars. 'Spit in their faces,' he said. 'Tell them to fuck their mothers.'

The phrase was like a blow. Instinctively, Tariq checked the doorway.

Rahim coughed long and hard. His face turned red as he wiped his mouth with a handkerchief. 'Do what you have to do,' Rahim said when he'd recovered, his voice rough. 'You won't regret it. Besides, it's the only choice you have. And if anyone gives you any trouble, just let me know.'

Rahim picked up the oud and carried it to the living room. He laid it on the sofa and opened its case. On the shelf beneath the window were family photographs arranged around a porcelain bowl.

He put the oud in the case and snapped it shut. 'I won't say anything more.'

As he left the house he asked Tariq, 'Is there anything I can do for you?'

'You could give a message to my parents.'

He nodded.

'Tell them to get off my fucking case?'

Rahim's eyebrows lifted but his eyes were soft. He smiled. 'All right,' he said. 'Though maybe not in so many words.'

Chapter 12

TARIQ rode his bike to Hawthorne Row and locked it in the rack outside Starbucks. School was in session, so he did not worry about meeting any classmates, but he kept an eye out for his mother, who sometimes came this way to buy flowers. The street had lost its summery edge; the storefronts were darker, the plants in the hanging baskets less colourful. Across the road, city workers carried leaf-blowers like machine guns, clearing the strips of lawn that ran between the sidewalks and the millrace.

He bought a box of reeds at the music store and descended the steps to Jamal's shop. The front door was locked tight, no note displayed. Hands cupped to the dusty window, he peered inside. The place looked abandoned. Balled-up clumps of paper lay in the main aisle.

Russell was not in the coffee shop, and the woman serving did not even know who Jamal was. Tariq cycled home. Scrolling through the call register on his phone, he found Jamal's number. It rang for a long time before a blurred voice answered.

'Jamal?'

'Who wants to know?'

'This is Tariq.' Silence. 'The clarinet player.'

'Oh yeah. Liquorice stick man.'

His voice was cracked and distant, as if he had just woken. It was two in the afternoon.

'I was at your store. How come you're closed?'

'Long story.'

'I'm looking for some Duke Ellington CDs. I've been, you know, trying to play some stuff by him.'

'Can't go wrong with the Duke.'

The way Jamal spaced his words was odd. No tightness, no energy. He did not sound like the man behind the counter rattling the glass top with a drumstick.

'Are you going to open today?'

'Ain't you in school now?'

'I'm on a break. Practising music.'

Sounds of something being moved, a muffled thud, a train whistle in the background. Sniffles and a noisy clearing of the throat. 'Look,' he said, 'why don't you come out here?'

'Where?'

'My place. I got plenty Ellington shit around here. And you can play for me.'

'Now?'

'You got something better to do?'

He gave Tariq the address.

'I'll cycle out. It'll take me a half hour or so.'

'Don't forget your axe.'

THE house was on the west side, in a neighbourhood like the one Tariq imagined Brad lived in: dirt yards, junked cars, cracked sidewalks seamed with weeds. Weathered houses with the shades drawn and trailer homes here and there, though Jamal lived in a solid bungalow with vinyl siding and a chain-link fence.

Tariq approached slowly. Small birds flitted aimlessly about the eaves. From the high weeds of the neighbouring house, a ginger cat watched them, paw raised. Pop bottles and old shoes littered the porch, and the screen door mesh was ripped from top to bottom. Behind the front-door glass was a flag in stripes of green, red and yellow, with the head of a lion roaring at the centre.

Jamal let him in without a word. The rooms were messy: scruffy furniture supporting piles of magazines and newspapers, clothes scattered on the floor, dusty lampshades, an old turntable surrounded by stacks and stacks of records. Smells of coffee and incense. Unframed posters of jazz musicians on the walls and jazz on the stereo. '*Such Sweet Thunder*,' Jamal told him. Ellington inspired by Shakespeare.

'You *do* know who Shakespeare is, don't you?'

'We're studying *Hamlet* in English.'

'Glad to hear it. No accounting for the ignorance of the youth of today. No offence.'

Since the phone call, Jamal had regained his verve. But he was jittery. His head and chin had a shadow of stubble. He wore white linen trousers held in place by a drawstring and a black T-shirt with a line drawing of a saxophonist. The stump of his arm was exposed, pink-streaked and puckered, moving jerkily as he talked, as if with a life of its own.

He cleared a spot on a stained sofa and gestured to Tariq to sit down. Cued a new track on the record. 'Listen and learn,' he said and went into the kitchen.

The music was stately. A clarinet rising and falling against a slow march of horns. Almost classical in its structure, but with that jazz feel. Jamal returned with coffee and a Coke and stayed quiet until the tune was over.

'Something, huh?'

'Awesome,' Tariq said.

'Jimmy Hamilton. Southern boy who grew up in Philadelphia. Like Trane. Thing about him is, he's cool. No funk. But swings like a motherfucker.'

'Not sure I know what you mean.'

'You will.' He sipped his coffee. Turned pensive. 'I should be at work. Day be for *selling*.'

'So why aren't you?'

'At war with the city,' he said. 'They claim I owe back taxes.'

'You don't?'

He grew agitated. 'Let me explain something. I pay my way. Always have. But when I see my money go immoral, I keep it in my pocket. City wants to put an incinerator on conservation land, I say fuck that, excuse my French.'

He wiped the corners of his mouth with his wrist.

'I'll let you in on a little secret,' he continued. 'Ain't just city taxes. I ain't paid federal taxes either, not since I left the service. What do you think about that?'

'How do you get away with it?'

'Guess what the defence budget is. Annual.'

'I don't know. Millions of dollars.'

'Millions? Shit. Seven hundred *billion*. Think about *that* number. Let's say you went to every man, woman and child in the country and took two grand off each of them. *That* be seven hundred billion. Every year. And everyone pays. Except me. *I do not pay no federal taxes*. And I will not till we out of the Middle East. Lock, stock and barrel.'

The record had ended. Birds chirped outside the windows. Jamal's face had gone hard and one sandalled foot was twitching. Tariq lifted the clarinet case to the sofa. 'Can I play something?'

Jamal shook off his distraction. 'Shoot.'

Tariq played the opening of 'In a Sentimental Mood'. After Jimmy Hamilton, it sounded tinny and stiff. And his fingers wouldn't move as they were meant. He had lost control of them, like a pitcher who turns wild in a close game.

When he was finished, Jamal stayed quiet for a while before saying, 'Last time we met, you said you'd play me some Iraqi stuff. What did you call it?'

'*Choubi.*'

'Yeah. Give me some of that.'

He played 'Mother, Here's My Beauty'. At a furious tempo, but straight through, with no mistakes. No problem. Natural as walking.

Jamal tapped his foot, smiled. 'I can dig *that*,' he said afterwards. 'You played it like you owned it.'

'I guess I just don't find it that interesting any more.'

'Well, let me tell you something. You know it. You feel it. You want to play jazz, you gotta feel it. Listen, my man, listen. Over and over. And keep practising.'

If only Mr Broquist had been so direct. Jamal sat in a wicker chair, legs spread wide, intense but relaxed, looking like a man who couldn't care less about what anyone thought. Someone who knew his own mind. Someone who might understand Tariq's troubles.

Jamal said, 'Still playing hooky?'

'I was never playing hooky.'

'No?'

Tariq's stomach fluttered. Maybe this was why he had come. To confess. 'I got suspended,' he said.

'Ah. So we ain't talking about being sick no more.'

Tariq shook his head. He told the story slowly, starting with the taunts in gym class, the incident in the parking lot, the comments on Facebook. When he got to the part about smoking reefer in the bathroom, Jamal snorted. But he said nothing and listened respectfully to the end.

When he'd finished, they sat silently for a while. A passing train clattered loudly, its whistle cleaving the air. The house must have been right next to the tracks.

Finally, Jamal spoke softly. 'My guess is, you seen worse where you come from.'

'It's different when it's you.'

'You can say that again. But these guys are punks. In Baghdad they be laughed at.'

'We're not in Baghdad.'

Jamal pinched the bridge of his nose and grimaced. 'I know the type,' he said. 'All mouth in the barracks, and when the shit start to rain down they the first to run.'

'Yeah, well, it's not like there's a war on. No shit *to* rain on them except what Ms Wessell says.'

Jamal continued as if Tariq had not spoken. 'Giving local people a hard time, like *they* ain't the victims. Hearts and minds, my ass. Some of these crackers, they be looking to waste anyone they can. Women. Kids. I told you some of the things I seen, you wouldn't believe it.'

His voice had lost any joy.

'I thought we were talking about Monroe High,' Tariq said.

'The world. I'm talking about the world. People the same everywhere. Put a little pressure on a man, you see what he's made of.'

Tariq decided to flow with the change of subject. 'Were you in Baghdad?' he asked.

Agitated, Jamal stood, moving on the balls of his feet. 'Fallujah. Operation Phantom Fury.' He paced from door to window and back, peering out with his shoulders hunched, as if besieged. 'God, those codenames. Such bullshit.'

'When?'

'The worst time. November 04. Marines went in and kicked butt, Army mopped up. And they weren't taking no prisoners, believe you me, not after what happened to those Blackwater cats.

I was with a team guarding a bridge on the north side of the town. Me and three others. Good guys. But some of the troops were absolute psychos. Shit, you saw it every day. Guys running .50-calibres like they was at target practice. Pancaking buildings, forget about who was inside. Every moving vehicle destroyed in case it was a suicide bomber. Operations officer told us not to worry about civilians being killed, they had a compensation fund. A fucking *compensation* fund.'

He was shaking. His voice droned but was full of tension. The creases at the back of his neck glistened with sweat.

'Main base was five, six klicks outside of town. The Alamo, we called it. It was, like, maybe you didn't feel so safe inside, but you still felt a whole lot safer than *outside*. Being on the streets was a nightmare. Every minute be eating into your stomach. Our detail had an armoured Humvee. Me and my buddies up front. Other cat name of Billingsley manning the rear. I didn't know him before, but he was all right. I was the driver.'

He exhaled slowly, raised his trembling hand to his mouth. 'Can't even get a driver's licence now because of this.' He waved the stump of his arm. 'But I drove and Jeff and Tony, they watched the road. Billingsley at the back with an M2, my guys beside me with M16s. Took a different route every day, to and from the bridge. Had to. Insurgents laying down IEDs every which way, you had to make sure you weren't predictable.'

He moved to the back window, stared unmoving at the high grass and broken fence behind the house. 'Anyways, the day comes, the day you hope you never see. A dead goat in the road, we know what that means, so I drive around it real careful like I always do, everybody on full alert. But this time it's a decoy and we're driving right into their trap. Bomb ain't in the carcase, it's in the ditch. Wheels roll over it and off it goes. Catches the passenger side full force and flips us. Jeff, he's gone. Instantly. Tony, blinded. Me, this.'

He waggled the stump and stopped talking. The chatter of birds in the back yard was tropical. Huge as he was, Jamal looked diminished before the window, slumped and shaking. Tariq wanted to be out back with the long grass and birdsong, but he sat quietly, waiting for the next move. When Jamal turned around, his face was stony. Tears streaked his cheeks.

'I'm sorry,' Tariq said.

Jamal waved away the words, wiped his face. 'Come here.'

Tariq followed him to a small room at the rear of the house. Above a washer and dryer was a cupboard secured with a fat padlock. Jamal fished a key from his pocket, unlocked it and opened wide the doors. Several guns hung on clips at the rear of the cupboard. Blue-black, gleaming, redolent of oil and shaved metal.

Jamal said nothing. He had stopped shaking. A strange force shimmered in the air. A closeness between them, a sharing of secrets. Tariq was frightened, then relieved when Jamal closed the doors and set the padlock back in place.

In the living room Jamal took a record from the pile and put it on the turntable. Before playing it, he said, 'What I just showed you, that's like your ace in the hole. The card you never want to play. You think the feeling it gives you is peace, but you're wrong. It's power. *This*,' he said, pointing at the record, 'is peace.'

A Love Supreme, by John Coltrane. He cued the opening section. The bang of a gong. A simple, four-note figure, repeated on bass like a mantra. Big chords on the piano. Then Coltrane coming in with that huge saxophone sound and wrenching tone, scattering notes like a Gatling gun, playing variations full of pain and gratitude and joy. Continuing trancelike until the whole room felt suspended outside of time and space. By the close, when the notes had evolved into a chant (Jamal, eyes shut tight, shouting along with the record: *a love su-preme, a love su-preme*), Tariq felt as he knew he was supposed to feel in mosque, but never did: uplifted, cleansed, released.

Jamal lifted the needle from the record. 'St John Coltrane,' he said quietly. He returned the record to its sleeve. He rummaged and found a CD version and handed it to Tariq. 'It's time,' he said. 'Go home. Listen to the whole thing. Empty your soul and listen.'

Tariq nodded, slipped the CD into his backpack. Outside, he unlocked his bike as Jamal stood on the porch. The ginger cat watched them from the long grass, still as a tiger. Jamal waved, flashed the peace sign.

As he cycled home, all Tariq could think about were the guns.

Chapter 13

THE WEEKS that followed were like a cold sleep. Because Tariq would not explain his actions, the school authorities suspended him for a month. They had no choice, they said. It was policy. And they reserved the right to expel him at the end of it. Yet he was required to keep pace with his studies, and a courier arrived each afternoon with notes from his teachers and homework assignments. Though he attended mosque with his parents and said prayers privately with the imam, there was no communication with his family. His sin was like a shield. They could not understand his silence, and though they grounded him until further notice, it was as if he now had power over them. Even Rahim kept his distance.

He was safe at last. Sealed in. His life took refuge in narrow spaces: his bedroom, his laptop, the occasional risky trip to the music store or Jamal's house when his parents were at work. During the day he listened to the new Coltrane and practised. Evenings were tense, and he retreated to his room early. He tried to write a poem about his feelings, but no words would come.

When his parents had gone to bed, he went online. He avoided Facebook or other sites where he might come across his schoolmates. Headphones on, he watched YouTube music and dance videos, jazz performances and streamed TV shows: stories of gangsters and drug lords and casual urban death. In the late hours he played fighting and escape games.

At two or three in the morning he would creep downstairs and pour himself a bowl of cereal. He ate in the chill kitchen, listening to the house's night sounds: gurgling pipes, unidentified creaks and rustles, the scrape of branches on the roof. The weather had turned cold. The windows rattled. Above the stove, blue and cream tiles formed a dense checkerboard pattern; if he stared long enough it would shift and pulse like an optical illusion and the negative image would hang in his retina long after he had looked away.

One night he was slowly padding back to his room when he heard a high-pitched cry. At first he thought it was an animal outside. Knocks and grunts and more cries, and with stark disgust he realised that his parents were having sex just a few feet away, nothing between him and them but the thin wooden panel of their door. He hurried into his room, clamped on his headphones, and listened to Duke Ellington at full volume.

Eventually he went to bed but couldn't sleep. He got up, turned on lamp and laptop, and idly surfed the Internet. He didn't dare leave the room. The moon hung in his window, alien, discoloured, telephone wires slicing across its face. The night was still and windless.

His phone, on silent, lit up. He checked his clock. Three-thirty in the morning. It was a text message from an unknown number. He stared at the phone for several minutes before opening the message: *you can run but you cant hide. we got your number freak.*

He sat, sweating, in his chair. Night ground slowly on its great black axis, moment to moment, while despair swished through the silence like a sword. Images riffled in his head as he searched for something, anything, to hold on to. Nothing was adequate to the emptiness, not music, not self, not love.

He typed 'I want to end it all' into Google. Most of the hits thrown up were suicide hotlines and articles about celebrities in high-profile meltdown, but nestled among the links was a forum of voices that matched the shouting in his head:

> i get made fun of because im gothic and fat. im 17 and have had depression for a few years now. i get thoughts of killing myself all the time. i have cut once before. i dont cut any more but i do other stuff that could hurt me i try not to but i cant help it. i cant get rid of the thoughts to kill myself. help please - ihatemylife

> The 4 reasons i want 2 die, heres pritty much all them – because of my mom, my boyfriend being an ass, my friends getting into fights with my other friends, and then them throwing me in the middle of it. I already typed my suicide letter. – melanie

After a few minutes of helpless browsing in the bad grammar and self-pity, Tariq found this:

> I'm 18 and I didn't really know any reasons why I should stay alive. Pray to Allah everyone said but what if you pray and he doesn't listen? I needed someone to talk to. I went on to Facebook and they have a fuck Islam group with like thousands of members. Just like my school. They wld all be happy if I killed myself. Finally I found a place where people like me can talk. With no hatred for who I am. – syrianboy

The post had a link that brought Tariq to a blog on topics related to young men and the Middle East. He surfed that site for a while, hitting random links until he came across a bulletin board called 'My Jihad'. To access the site he had to register and receive a password by email. He used the name *a_love_supreme*. When he logged on, it was as if he had been dropped into a movie. Most of the postings were in Arabic, but several were in English:

The hand of Allah is always on his sword.

I'm just waiting for the time when they don't have any idea when its coming and then they'll be sorry they ever said anything about what they know is sacred to me and all my people. As the Qur'an says, O men of understanding, that you may guard yourselves.

Yea! if you remain patient and are on your guard, and they come upon you in a headlong manner, your Lord will assist you with five thousand havoc-wreaking angels.

The language, so familiar in its sound and shape, had never been so clear to him. A great calmness settled on his soul. The poem he had been searching for now came. He did not need to compose it. It flowed from his fingers like a prayer he had known all his life:

I have been shown the sword
on it, my name
a light shone from the top of the hill
and on the blade I saw not the blood of my grandparents
but the mark of my enemies

Within minutes he had a response, from *allahisgreat*:

If your cause is righteous then you are obliged. Do what you must.

He went to bed. His hands tingled.

THE next afternoon an unstamped letter for him arrived through the mail slot. It was handwritten on lavender paper.

Hey Tariq

I'm sorry for not being in touch. I guess I thought you needed some space. And I appreciate that you are probably not answering your phone right now. Though to be honest, I haven't called. I'm sorry about that.

I may as well start with the funny stuff. When news got out about you being busted, Annalise absolutely <u>freaked</u>. You know what she's like anyway, and when this news hit her she got so incredibly paranoid. She thought for sure she was going to be next, I guess you know why. She's calmed down by now, but it was hilarious while it lasted.

So what is going on with you? Are you deliberately trying to ruin everything? I don't want to sound like that loon Wessell, but what about your college applications? Your music? Does this mean you won't be playing at Thanksgiving? I'm so bummed about this whole thing. I miss you, too.

I'm thinking you could use somebody to talk to right about now.

Call me?

Always your friend,

Rachel

'Freaked.' Underlined. How could that be chance?

THE night after Halloween the mosque held a special prayer service for peace. Congregants from the Shia madressah in Verona were invited. This wasn't the new madressah of Africans, but a well-established congregation, mostly Middle Eastern families.

Many had business contacts with members of the Masjid As-Sunnah mosque.

After the service, Tariq saw Yusef standing on the steps to the prayer hall with his father and younger brother, all dressed in *dishdashas* and skullcaps. Malik, it turned out, knew Yusef's father, who ran a hospital supply business in Milwaukee. They spoke for a while and moved towards the dining hall. Yusef told the others that he and Tariq would follow them in a few minutes.

The night was cool but still. From where he stood, Tariq could see the minaret, vaguely outlined against the night sky, the crescent moon glinting at its peak, and the twisted iron railings that enclosed the sacred property. In spite of the autumn chill, the juniper bushes and chrysanthemums were fragrant. Sufi musicians who had been invited for the evening remained in the prayer hall, playing religious music on reed flutes. The sound was thin and mysterious.

'How are you?' Yusef said.

'What are they saying about me?'

'Who?'

'In school.'

'I don't listen.'

'You must hear something,' Tariq said.

'Nothing they say means anything to me. Their world and this one' – Yusef swept his hand in a semicircle, taking in the mosque and its grounds – 'they're completely opposite.'

The light from the prayer hall fell across his beard, making him look older. Laughter and the sounds of recited Arabic floated above the strains of the flutes.

When Tariq didn't reply, Yusef continued. 'You are lucky. You have a beautiful prayer hall. A proper school. Our mosque is a converted office.'

'The building doesn't matter. Like the imam says, it's what's in your heart.'

'No, it matters. What people see. What they think.'

'About us?'

'Of course.'

Yusef drew close and dropped his voice. 'You're right not to return to Monroe High.'

'That's not what my father thinks.'

'He doesn't go there. He doesn't know. If I didn't have my college application to worry about I wouldn't be there. You should come here. To your mosque school. Get a *real* education.'

'I don't know.'

'If you came here you'd have respect. You wouldn't be pushed around. You'd be part of a majority.'

Yusef had never been so friendly to Tariq. So respectful.

A man walked out of the prayer hall and greeted Yusef. He wore an aqua silk robe, embroidered with red thread at the sleeves and neckline, and a white knitted skullcap. He stopped to put on his shoes and then stared at Tariq.

'Hey. It's the soccer star.'

It was Sahar Nassam, the guy with the smooth manner and expensive jewellery who had stood up to Tariq's father and Mahmoud Khan at the soccer match.

'You went crazy that day,' Sahar said.

'What's this?' Yusef said.

'This kid here has a temper. We were playing football against those Africans from Az-Zahra and he lost it. Went after his old man.'

'I was just having a bad day,' Tariq said.

Sahar smiled. 'Hey, no need to apologise. No disrespect to your father, but some men still think they're living in the old country.'

Tariq would not have expected Sahar to show up here, and certainly not in traditional dress. At the match he had made a show of being an ordinary American, with his Wisconsin accent and fashionable clothes and IT job in Kenosha.

'Tariq's been having a few bad days lately,' Yusef said.

'Oh yeah? How so?'

When Tariq didn't say anything, Yusef told the story of the bullying and suspension. Tariq stared at the ground.

'There's nothing to be ashamed of,' Sahar said when he had finished. 'This sort of thing goes on all the time. If you wait for the school to take action, what do you think they'll do? Nothing. This is the situation we all face. Every day. A hundred years ago it was the Irish and Italians who got the suspicion. Now it's Arabs. What did the Irish do? They protected themselves. They helped each other out.'

'I'm not Irish.'

'No. You are an Arab. And what those pigs did to you? It's a hate crime. Believe me. But it happens every day. They attacked you and it was racially motivated, right?'

'I guess.'

'You *guess*.'

Sahar looked at Yusef.

'Not only this incident,' Yusef said. 'There are things said in that school every day that are insulting. Ethnic slurs and comments that make you feel ashamed. And it's getting worse. Ramadan this year was very difficult.'

He bowed his head.

'There are laws forbidding their behaviour,' Sahar said. 'But when people don't obey the law, other action is necessary.' From his wallet he took a business card. 'Those animals who are mistreating you? I know people who can take care of it so they never bother you again. Believe me. People like us.'

Several women, including Tariq's mother, had come out from the dining hall and were beckoning those still outside to come in for the evening meal. There was a smell of roast lamb.

Sahar handed the card to Tariq. 'When you're ready to do something about it, give me a call.'

Chapter 14

RAHIM fell ill. The doctors did not know what was wrong. He had internal bleeding and bad headaches. He had to give up work and was in and out of hospital. Leyla was not taking it well. Malik and Zaida took turns staying at their house and Tariq was on his own more than ever.

After dinner one evening, as Tariq was leaving the table, his mother said, '*Habibi*?'

'Yes?'

'Yes what?'

'Yes, Ommi,' he said.

Malik was with Rahim. The room smelled of spices. Warm, dry air from the heating vent wafted against Tariq's skin. They had turned on the furnace for winter.

'Did you do your homework?'

'I'm going to do it now.'

His mother stood up and carried her plate to the sink. Her shoulders sagged. Her back to him, she said, 'Were you riding your bike today?'

'Today?'

'Yes. Near the old railway station.'

'Ommi, I'm grounded.'

She faced him. 'That's not what I asked you.'

That afternoon he had three missed calls from her number. He should have known something was up. Still, the question had taken him unawares.

'No,' he said, staring at her. 'I was here. All day.'

She nodded and stepped back to the table and gathered the soiled tablecloth. Though they'd had an early dinner, the windows were dark. Dusk had fallen, the hour when ordinary objects become difficult to identify.

'How is Ammu Rahim?' he asked.

'It's hard to say.'

'Can I go see him?'

'Not just now,' she said.

'Why, because I'm grounded?'

Her eyes were glassy. Her bottom lip was tight, her chin a pucker of wrinkles. 'I'm going to need you,' she said.

'What do you mean?'

'And your father... he's going to need you, too.'

Alarmed, Tariq pushed his chair against the table so that the legs scraped the floor with a whine. 'Do you mean because of Rahim? Is it that bad?'

She looked away.

'Why can't I see him, Ommi?'

Weeping, she motioned him to leave. 'Go do your homework,' she said.

HE saw Jamal almost every day. The store remained closed, but they met in the coffee shop or at Jamal's house or they walked along the railway tracks as far as the grain elevators behind the fairground. They talked about music mostly, but also politics and religion and what Jamal called the conspiracy of the powerful. Or rather Jamal talked. Tariq listened carefully, bobbing in the wake of the man's energy, the big voice and strong opinions.

One afternoon Tariq arrived on his bike and saw Jamal on his porch struggling with the door.

'Goddamn it,' Jamal shouted.

He slammed the door so hard the glass shook. He stuck the key in the lock but without a second hand to pull the handle tight he couldn't manage.

'Can I help?'

Jamal didn't answer, but Tariq reached around him, grasped the doorknob and pulled hard. The key turned easily.

Jamal scowled. 'Weather changes and the wood warps,' he said. 'These old houses.'

'Where are you going?'

'I got business to attend to.'

'To do with the store?'

Stiffly, Jamal walked down the porch steps. He was jittery, distracted. He wore a denim jacket, its loose sleeve coffee-stained, and his pants were creased and worn. Over his shoulder was a plastic airlines bag with an out-of-date Delta Airlines logo.

He leaned over at the waist and peered up the road. 'Said ten minutes.'

As the trees lost their leaves and the November rains fell, Jamal's street had turned bare and tawdry. The street gutters were sticky with grey mud. Some of the houses still had Halloween decorations in the windows, cardboard cutouts of black cats and flying witches.

A yellow cab pulled up, an old Ford with speckled bumpers and sagging shocks. The driver looked like a Russian holy man.

As Jamal climbed in, Tariq said, 'Should I come?'

'Don't make no difference to me.'

They drove to an even worse part of town, west of the railroad tracks and the abandoned quarry and onto the loop road around the back of the lake, where most people lived in trailers and properties were guarded by short-haired dogs on long chains.

They turned on to a dirt road lined with pine trees and stopped at a trailer with a FOR SALE sign nailed to a fencepost. Jamal motioned Tariq to come with him and told the driver to wait. In the window of the trailer was a sign with the words PSYCHIC SERVICES: PALM AND TAROT READINGS over a telephone number.

Jamal knocked on the screen door. They waited. He pulled open the screen and banged the inner door with his fist and shouted, 'Open up, Charmaine.'

Still no-one answered.

'Wait here,' Jamal said and walked over to the window. He peered in past the sign.

'Maybe I should get in the car,' Tariq said.

'Stay where you are. Anyone opens that door you shout.'

He went around the back. Some yelling came from inside and the front door flew open violently, nearly hitting Tariq in the face. A heavy woman in a velour track suit ran out, her faced screwed tight with rage. She carried a golf club. 'Where is he? *Jamal*!'

Tariq backed away quickly. Jamal came out from behind the trailer. The sleeve of his jacket caught on a low branch and he cursed and flailed until it loosened. Charmaine watched him, her free hand on her broad hip, her head tilted.

'I want to see my girl,' Jamal said.

'Is that so?'

'It's my right.'

'Well, you *wrong* about that. For sure. I got a copy of the restraining order, you want to re*fresh* your mind.'

'She's my baby.'

'She ain't no baby. She's twelve years old and she ain't here.'

'Where is she?'

'Now, that ain't none of your business.'

Beside the trees was a shed with a corrugated metal roof. Beside it was a rusted pick-up truck. Faded newspaper and bits of Styrofoam lay scattered at Jamal's feet.

He moved towards her.

'*Daryl*,' she shouted, hefting the seven iron.

'I'm here.'

A huge man filled the trailer door. Jamal took him in. Dirty T-shirt. Tattoos. Belly hanging over his belt like a bag of rice, but powerful in the chest and mean around the mouth.

'So you got yourself a bodyguard,' Jamal said. 'How 'bout it, Daryl? The pussy you getting worth all the grief?'

Charmaine screamed and raised the golf club. Jamal lunged and grabbed it from her and tossed it to his right. The head of the club hit one of the pick-up's headlights and broken glass tinkled to the ground. Daryl stepped out from the door. 'You asshole,' he said.

Jamal unzipped the airline bag and everyone froze. The taxi driver started his engine.

'I want to see Naima,' Jamal said.

His hand was inside the bag. The cabbie was having trouble getting the car into reverse.

'Lester,' Jamal shouted at him, 'don't you be going nowhere. Tariq, tell him to stay where he is, he wants to get paid.'

Tariq got into the back seat of the taxi. Jamal and Charmaine and Daryl stood alert and primed for the next scene, like characters in a play.

'You heard the woman,' Daryl said carefully, watching the airline bag. 'Your girl isn't here. So just go on back the way you come and we'll forget this ever happened.'

'It's my right. She's my daughter.'

'Nobody's arguing with you on that point,' Daryl said. 'But she isn't here. And don't none of us want something stupid to happen, you with me on that?'

Jamal hiked the bag up his shoulder, kept his hand where it was. Cleared his throat and sniffed. 'You tell her I came by, Charmaine. You tell her I want to see her. I got a right.'

'I'll tell her,' Charmaine said. But her face was tight as a bulldog's.

Slowly, Jamal crossed the littered yard and joined Tariq in the back seat. The taxi left with a spray of gravel. Jamal withdrew his hand from the bag and zipped it tight.

'Goddamn it, Jamal,' the driver said, looking at him in the rear-view mirror, 'what kind of damn-fool bullshit was that?'

Jamal didn't reply. He sat in the car like a man leaving home for good, staring at dead wood tangled on the lakefront and faded campaign posters of local politicians on the telephone poles.

The driver fiddled with the radio knobs and settled on a pop station.

'Lester,' Jamal said, rubbing his forehead.

'What?'

'Turn that shit off.'

At the house Jamal went into his bedroom and stayed there for a long time. While Tariq waited, his phone rang, surprising him. He thought he had switched it off. It was his mother. He let it ring out. She called again. In a panic, he answered.

'Where are you?' she said.

'At the house.'

'*I'm* at the house.'

'My friend's house.'

'What friend?'

'Just a friend.'

In the pause that followed, his heart beat in the receiver cupped to his ear.

'Come home now, Tariq,' she said calmly. 'We need to talk.'

'Where's Baba?'

'He's not here. And he won't be for a while. So come home.'

As Tariq gathered his things, Jamal emerged in different clothes. He moved slowly, head down, his bald pate dull beneath the low ceiling. His puffy eyes flickered, as if searching out cockroaches in the corners.

'You want some soda?' he said.

'I have to go, Jamal.'

'What's wrong?'

'Nothing. I have to meet my mother.'

Jamal looked away, then grasped Tariq's arm so hard it hurt. His face was ashen and lustreless.

Tariq said, 'What's the matter?'

'I haven't seen my baby in eight months. Since St Patrick's Day. Her school was in the parade in Milwaukee.'

He was fierce but vulnerable, like an animal caught in a trap.

'Marching in her little costume. Throwing a baton high in the air. Did my heart proud.'

'Does she live with Charmaine?'

Jamal let go of his arm. Shook his head. 'One day a week, usually. She's in a programme. Naima that is. Some kind of shit the state runs, whatever. Won't let me near her, that's all *I* know. And Charmaine, she keeps the day different so I don't cotton on.'

The thought of his mother waiting at home was like a gun in Tariq's face.

'You know what Naima means?' Jamal said.

'Isn't it a song by John Coltrane?'

Jamal smiled weakly. 'You learning, my man, you definitely learning. It means "peace". In Arabic.'

'I should know that.'

Tears streaked Jamal's cheeks, disappearing into the tufts of his goatee.

'I'll call you tonight,' Tariq said. 'I promise.'

Chapter 15

HIS MOTHER sat on the sofa, hands folded in her lap. Though she wore an American dress and no hijab, her posture was pure Iraqi: formal, erect, controlled.

She waited for Tariq to speak. 'Are you OK, Ommi?' he said.

'You tell me.'

'How is Rahim?'

'We'll talk about Rahim in a minute. Where were you?'

'I told you. At a friend's house.'

She thought about this. 'I'm going to make some tea,' she said. 'Hang up your jacket and wash yourself.'

In the living room, she poured the tea into small glass cups, the ones she used for special occasions, and dropped two cubes of sugar into each. The cups sat on her best silver tray. Clouds of steam rose between them. The intense fragrance of cardamom. They stirred the tea with tiny silver spoons.

'This friend,' his mother said. 'Is it a girl?'

'No, a man.'

She raised her eyebrows. 'A man? Who?'

'I met him when I was buying music. Before – all this happened. He has a shop on Hawthorne Row which the city is closing down. He's disabled and has problems. I'm helping him.'

'Is this another lie?'

'Another?'

'You told me you were not downtown on your bike. Now you

tell me you are helping some stranger. How do I know what to believe? Where is the trust?'

'It is the truth, Ommi. I swear by Allah.'

'So why are you helping this man? What are you doing for him?'

'I told you. He's disabled. He needs assistance and I'm helping him. It's my *zakat*.'

'*Zakat* is giving money to the poor.'

'The imam always says that if you don't have much money, then you can do good deeds instead. It's one of the Five Pillars of Islam.'

She smiled faintly. 'I know what it is, Tariq.'

They drank. The afternoon clouds had lifted and the sun slanted through the windows, lighting up the pink walls and the embroidered rugs. Though his mother was doing her best to appear calm and unworried, her face was worn and weary. There were problems at the university, of course. Rahim and Leyla. His own situation.

'Ommi, I'm doing my homework every day. Saying *salat*. Going to mosque.'

'And leaving the house. Without us knowing and against your father's command.'

'What good is it staying here every single minute? I need fresh air. Do you really think I can stay here all day, cooped up like a chicken?'

'This has been your choice, Tariq.'

Suddenly, pity for his mother gave way to a clotted feeling in his chest, a clenching of his heart. 'Do you think I would choose to go back to that school?' he said hoarsely. 'To be harassed and bullied?'

Her eyes flared in surprise. 'So it is so?'

He shook his head.

'Why are you shutting me out, *habibi*?' she said. 'What have I done?'

'You haven't done anything. It's me. I'm confused. I don't know what to do.'

The large clock above the door ticked in the silence and the refrigerator motor whinnied from the kitchen. In a strange way the house was alive for him, yet part of his confusion. He felt safer here than anywhere else, but he also felt as if in a prison.

'Speak to Baba,' his mother said. 'He will help you.'

'I don't think so.'

'He wants what's best for you.'

'What he wants is what's best for *himself*.'

Zaida pressed her hands together so hard her fingers turned white. Touched her face, smoothed her dress against the tops of her thighs. Poured more tea.

'Let me tell you something,' she finally said. Her voice had shifted register, as if beginning a prayer. 'Before I met your father, he was an intern at the Ibn Sina Hospital. Around the time Saddam took power. This was before the government took Ibn Sina over for the elite. Malik was still in medical school and he was a party member, but he was a committed socialist as well. He believed in working for the good of the people.

'Anyway, he was at the hospital in the summer of 1979, working eighteen-hour shifts, when Saddam became president and the whole country changed. You have no idea. It was bad before, but this was worse. The real problems began then, the problems still going on today. The purges. Kurds, Iranians, communists. Death squads. No-one was safe. You were always listening at night for a knock on the door. In July security forces came to the hospital and arrested him and put him in the Central Prison. He was not allowed any visitors. They beat him. Your grandparents, they didn't even know where he was. They were worried sick of course.'

She took a deep breath. Her hands shook in the late-afternoon light.

'Rahim found out where he was. The younger brother that the family always felt would never come to any good. He liked music and he liked, God forgive him, a few drinks. But he had a job repairing tanks for the army and he stole a colonel's uniform and went to the prison and bullied the guards until they let his brother go. Brought him home. Quit his job and nursed him for a month. *Habibi*, your uncle was twenty-one years old. He saved Baba's life.'

She lifted the tray of glasses and brought it to the kitchen. Tariq sat in the pink glow of the room, amid the lacquered boxes and brass candlesticks. She returned and stood beside the sofa like the imam before his congregation.

'I'd like to see Rahim,' Tariq said.

'Tomorrow, maybe. In the meantime, have you decided what to do?'

'About what?'

'You know.'

'Do you mean am I going to tell the principal what he wants to hear?'

'I mean that you have to make a decision. You have to stop drifting. What about college? Have you thought about how all this will affect your applications?'

'No.'

She leaned across and touched his head. Her hand was cool.

'Think of Baba,' she said. 'How much Rahim means to him and what he is going through. And whatever you do, remember: you only harm yourself by lying to your parents. Any lie is a lie before God.'

HIS father stayed with Rahim that night, so Tariq did not see him until the next day. His mother left early. Mid-morning he was listening to music in his bedroom when he heard the sudden booming of the television. He went downstairs. The shaded living room flashed with colour and light and the screen was tuned to Al Jazeera. Gesticulating wildly, an old imam spoke harshly in Arabic before a bank of microphones. His turban was dirty and his thick glasses made his eyes look twice their size.

Tariq turned down the sound. He went into the kitchen and found Malik, in his hospital clothes, slumped at the table, staring at the blue-and-cream checkerboard squares above the stove. For the first time that he could remember, Tariq was not afraid of his father but afraid *for* him. His baba looked broken. His face was wan, his hair tousled, the knot of his necktie loosened in a way that made his wattled neck look scrawny and vulnerable.

'Baba,' he said quietly.

His father's eyes flickered his way. He reached out to Tariq, who took his hand. It was as cold as a fish. 'Your ommi is with Rahim.'

'That's good,' Tariq said.

Malik remained silent.

'Would you like some tea, Baba?'

'Did you say *salat?*'

'Yes.'

'And you remembered Rahim?'

'Of course.'

His father's face crumpled quickly and completely, like a dry leaf thrown on the fire. He covered his eyes with his hands and sobbed, a single, wrenching stab of sound that made the hairs on Tariq's arms stand up. Instinctively, he moved towards his father, and then just as instinctively pulled back. He stood helplessly, arms at his sides.

Malik recovered himself, wiped his eyes. 'He's dying, Tariq.'

'Is he?'

His father's face tightened. 'Didn't I just say so?'

'I'm sorry, Baba.'

Malik lifted a finger, as if to remonstrate, lost his train of thought.

'Why don't I fix you something to eat?' Tariq said.

Though he looked as if he hadn't eaten in days, Malik dismissed the suggestion with a chopping motion of his hand. 'I'm going to bed. I'm exhausted and I have to be at the hospital at seven. Not that I'll get any sleep.'

He left the kitchen. Tariq drew back the curtains and poured himself some cereal and sat and ate it. Between the strokes of the spoon's scrape on the bowl, the clock ticked loudly.

Malik returned. He had taken off his shirt and tie. His mesh undershirt hung from his bony shoulders as if on a clothesline.

'Your mother said you have homework.'

'I'm going to do it now.'

Malik stared at his son open-mouthed, his shoulder dipped, as if one arm was heavier than the other. 'When is this business going to be resolved?'

'What business?' Tariq said.

'Are you going back to school or aren't you?'

'I was thinking,' Tariq said carefully, 'that I might go to the mosque school.'

His father straightened. 'Are you serious?'

'Yes.'

'Have you spoken to the imam?'

'No.'

Malik's face was scrunched up, as if he was working out a math problem. 'What makes you think they'd take you?' he said.

This last sentence was spoken with the old bitterness. Tariq sat still, cereal bowl poised on his lap, braced for whatever nastiness or violence his father might choose to unleash.

But Malik's face lost its hardness, as if he couldn't maintain the authority he had always claimed. 'Perhaps you could start after al-Hijra,' he said.

'Perhaps.'

He wavered in the doorway, his face haggard, his eyes sad, his shoulders thin as a bird's.

'I'm going to bed,' he said at last.

He went upstairs and Tariq went into the living room to watch Al Jazeera.

Chapter 16

ON THURSDAY, Tariq's mother stayed with Leyla. Malik was working an extended shift at the hospital. So after lunch, Tariq headed to Jamal's house with his clarinet. The case was too cumbersome to carry while cycling, so he wrapped the joints individually in kitchen towels and placed them carefully in his backpack along with his phone and two CDs.

Though the sun came and went, it was cold. He regretted not wearing gloves. He cycled through the centre of town and out along the millrace road. On this stretch, the canal banks were free of trees and bushes, and the ruffled water reflected the broken clouds. As he circled the old railway yard and approached the narrow humpbacked bridge, a passing car edged too close, forcing him to swerve. His front wheel hit the high kerb sidelong, sending him head over heels onto the canal bank. He broke the fall with his hands, but his knees hit the bridge's concrete skirting, ripping his pants. His backpack tore open so that the CDs and clarinet pieces scattered along the bank and the bell of the instrument fell into the stream.

Knees throbbing, he scrambled to the water's edge and plucked the grimy bell from the reeds. He cleaned it with a kitchen towel and returned it to the backpack. He gathered the other pieces, wiped them clean as best he could and climbed up the bank. He was dizzy and tearful. His back hurt and his hands were muddy and scratched. Blood seeped through the torn knees of his jeans.

The front tyre of his bike was so warped it would not revolve. He slung the backpack over his shoulder and, lifting the front wheel clear of the ground, pulled the bike along the sidewalk, limping back the way he had come. Dark birds skittered past at an odd angle, the ground beneath his feet undulated, a lone swan brightened and faded as clouds scudded past the sun. A ringing in his ears drowned out the birdcalls and traffic.

He didn't see the black Land Cruiser until it had stopped beside him. The passenger window lowered and he heard his name called. It was Rachel. He said nothing. She pulled in and put on her hazard lights. Still dazed, he set the bike down and stood unmoving on the sidewalk.

'What happened?' she called through the open window. 'Are you all right?'

When he still didn't answer she got out of the car. 'Oh my God, look at your knees. Here, get in.'

'What about the bike?'

'We'll put it in the back.'

She wanted to take him to her house, but he insisted that she drive him home. He struggled with the seatbelt, and she leaned across and helped him snap the buckle. Driving slowly, she looped back along Clearbrook Drive and followed the cross streets to his neighbourhood. The radio was tuned low to a rock station. The clouds had bulked up and a scatter of large raindrops blurred the windshield. Rachel leaned forward in the big front seat, peering past the wipers.

Again she asked what had happened. He cleared his throat and told her.

'Do you want to go to the clinic?'

'No. It's just scrapes and bruises.'

But he was overwhelmed with dizziness, as if on a cliff edge, frightened but tempted to leap. He steadied himself with a hand on the dashboard.

'I couldn't believe it when I saw you there,' she said.

She wiped condensation from the window with the back of her hand.

'You look different,' he said.

Her hair had been cut and neatly styled. She wore a blue-striped cotton blouse, a pencil skirt and black dress pumps. Heavy perfume. Around her neck was a thin silver chain and a star of David pendant.

'Where are your glasses?' he asked.

'I got contacts. Still getting used to them, to be honest.'

'Right.'

His hand had left a muddy print on the dashboard. He cleaned it with the sleeve of his shirt.

'I was on a college visit this morning,' she said. 'With my dad.'

'Where?'

'UW.'

'But you're a junior.'

'They have a summer honours programme. If I got into that I'd have an edge if I decided to apply next year.'

'I thought you wanted to go to Northwestern.'

'I do. But Madison has a good Jewish studies programme. My dad's big on it.'

They negotiated the quiet streets. American flags hung from most of the porches. The lawns glistened, the trees towered, red and gold. The interior of the Land Cruiser smelled of leather, plastic and the sweet musk of her perfume.

UW. Jewish studies. It was as if Tariq was circling the world in a space station, gazing down at canopies of cloud and drifting continents.

AT the house, she helped him lift the bike from the back of the Land Cruiser and carry it to the porch. The rain had strengthened. Next door, Mr Greenbriar, stooped and moustachioed, wrapped a garden hose around its reel as he watched them.

'I better go in, look after this,' he said, pointing at his knees.

'I'll help you.'

'That's OK.'

'*Tariq.*'

Staring down Mr Greenbriar, he said to her, 'Take off your shoes before you go inside.'

She had never been in his house. When they walked into the living room, she looked at the pink walls and laughed. 'Oh my God. What is this, a bordello?'

She circled the room, pressing the cushions, lifting the brass trays, testing the nap of the hanging rug with thumb and forefinger. In her stocking feet and new clothes she moved like a dancer.

'It's like Ali Baba and the Forty Thieves.'

He shrugged. 'Just a normal Iraqi house.'

'Right. In a normal Iraqi neighbourhood.'

He changed into shorts and a T-shirt and threw his muddy clothes into the laundry. He fetched bandages, towels and antiseptic cream from the bathroom. When he returned, she was in the kitchen with a basin of warm water and a washcloth.

'Sit,' she said.

Kneeling, she cleaned and dressed his wounds. As she worked, he could see the tops of her breasts inside the V of her blouse, the silver star of David dangling in the dark space between them. He fixed his gaze on the dripping faucet but could not help stealing glances. The rich smell of her hair mingled with the spice of her perfume. Her hand grazed the bottom of his bare thigh as she wrapped gauze around his knee. His breathing thickened and he started to go hard. Closing his eyes, he silently recited the *Tashahhud*: Salutations to God and prayers and good deeds... And so he controlled himself.

He cut slices of poppy-seed cake and made mint tea, which they drank from glass cups. She ate primly, holding a paper napkin beneath her chin to catch falling crumbs. Her eyes were a deeper hazel than he remembered, flecked with green, and he wondered if her new contacts were tinted. They ate silently, listening to the tick of the clock and the patter of rain on the window. The accident, the rescue, the intimacy of their moments here in the house made him light-headed and prone to tears. Her dark colouring and Semitic features were familiar and comforting and recalled feelings that came before memory.

They sorted through the stained clarinet pieces. Several keys were crooked. Some pads were missing. He bent the keys back into place and tried to recall where he had left his spare pads. But one of the joints had a crack in the wood, so he put everything aside, knowing he would have to bring in the instrument for repair.

He felt inside the backpack and checked all the pockets.

'Shit,' he said.

'What?'

'I lost my phone. It must still be down there.'

'We can go back.'

All sense of purpose drained from him. Leaning on his elbows over the empty glass, he rested his head on his fingertips. Tears dripped from his cheeks onto the plate. Rachel reached across the table and squeezed his shoulder. With a shudder he took a deep breath and went into the living room. She followed him and they sat side by side on the sofa.

'I guess it's all been hard for you,' she said.

'I don't know why. It's just a stupid phone.'

'But it's not the phone.'

'No.'

The shower had passed and the sun streamed through the window behind them. Their shoeless feet lined the polished floor like birds on a wire. His bandaged knees jutted into the mote-filled space absurdly.

'Where were you going? When you crashed.'

'No place. Just taking a ride.'

'You're allowed out?'

'Not really.'

'What do you do all day?'

'Watch TV. Do homework. Wessell still sends it. And I play. *Did* play. Before I smashed my stupid clarinet.'

Her eyes narrowed.

'You probably know that Josh Hall is playing your part at the Thanksgiving concert,' she said.

'No, I didn't. Do you still hang out with him?'

'I never hung out with him.' She sighed and swivelled on the sofa so that she faced him. She touched his arm. 'It's *you* I want to hang out with. Why do you keep pushing me back?'

For almost a year he had wished for such a moment: when she would declare, plainly, that she liked him in a certain way, that she thought they were right for each other. When she would offer him a chance to declare how he felt about her.

So why didn't he answer her?

'And when are you coming back to school?' she said at last.

'I don't know.'

'How can you not know?'

'I'm on indefinite suspension.'

'Until when?'

'Until I tattle-tale.'

She raised her eyebrows. The contacts, the new clothes, the trimmed and styled hair – it was as if she were an adult, he the guilty child, defending himself.

'Tell them what went on with Jorgensen?' she said. 'Is that what you mean?'

'That's just it. Nothing went on.'

She stood up. 'Bullshit, Tariq. That asshole's been picking on you for a year. You've been terrified. You *told* me, like, how many times?'

'And I don't want him picking on me for the next year. And the year after that.'

'And how do you think you're going to get him to stop?'

'Not by ratting him out, that's for sure.'

'"Ratting him out"? What is this, the Mafia?'

'Shut up, Rachel.'

'So you admit he's still bullying you.'

He stood to face her eye to eye, but the dizziness returned and he had to steady himself against the wall before lurching into the kitchen.

He leaned over the sink.

'What's the matter?' she said, behind him.

'Nothing. I don't want to talk about this any more. It doesn't make any difference, anyway. I'm not going back. Whether they want me or not. I've decided.'

'Not going back to school? You have to.'

'No, I don't.'

'You have to go somewhere.'

He wheeled around. 'I'm going to the mosque school.'

She stared at him, open-mouthed. 'What? When?'

'January. After al-Hijra.'

She shook her head, lost for words.

'Don't look at me like that,' he said. 'You go to Hebrew school.'

'Yeah, on Wednesday afternoon. For two hours. Like you go to mosque on Friday. But I don't buy into the whole fundamentalist shtick. The us and them. The intolerance. And neither do you. How many times have we talked about this?'

Everything she said he agreed with. Or had agreed with.

And now everything she said enraged him. He grew flushed. 'Like I said, I don't want to talk about it.'

'That's no answer.'

'I just want to be left alone. I want to go somewhere where I can think for myself. Where I'm not always looking over my shoulder.'

'Like the mosque school's going to let you think for yourself?'

'At least I won't be called a freak.'

'No, you'll *be* a freak. Memorising the Qur'an all day. Telling women what they can and can't wear. If you ever *see* a woman.' Her eyes blazed.

'So who's being intolerant now?' he said quietly.

Her expression wavered.

'And I'm not a freak,' he said.

'I know. I'm sorry.'

'Maybe the best thing would be if you left.'

She slid across the hardwood floor in her socks, opened the door, put on her shoes and was gone.

He watched her car pull away, stunned. Where had the words he had said come from? They were the opposite of all he believed. All he felt.

Or were they?

He put the damaged bike in the garage where it couldn't be seen, dressed in pants that covered his bandages and waited for his parents to come home.

Chapter 17

THE DIGITAL GLOW said 3:35. Darkness. Urgent voices. A rush of feet in the hallway.

Tariq went downstairs. At the front door his father was putting on his jacket. His greying, uncombed hair rose from his brow like a bush. Zaida stood beside him in her bathrobe, a hand to her mouth.

'What's the matter?' Tariq said.

She crossed the living room and embraced him. 'Baba has to go to the hospital.'

'For work?'

'Not Monroe General. The Deaconess. Rahim is not well.'

Malik sifted through the contents of a bowl beside the door. 'Where are my keys? Zaida. My *keys*.' His voice was fragile and alien.

Zaida searched her handbag for her own set.

Tariq stepped forward. 'I want to go.'

'Not possible,' his father said without looking at him.

Tariq looked at his mother. 'Ommi.'

Malik thrust his hand out. 'The keys, the keys!'

'Malik,' she said, 'he's right. We should all go. The three of us.'

'There's no time.'

She hefted the keys. Considered. 'We'll be ready in a minute,' she said.

TARIQ had never been on the streets at this hour. The traffic lights flashed amber in the empty gloom. The occasional taxi or milk truck floated past like a hearse. His throat had the taste of interrupted sleep, dry and salty. In the cramped rear seat of his father's Toyota, his sore knees bumped the seat ahead of them whenever Malik touched the brakes. At each stop or start or turn, his father made a small, unconscious groan, as if pushing a stone up a hill.

The hospital, however, was hectic with noise and light. The crowd in the emergency department was divided evenly between those rushing about as if panicked and those, like Tariq and his parents, who waited for news. While Malik spoke to the admitting nurse, Tariq watched the flow of arriving patients, the pale faces of those who brought them in, the reflective gleam of the specialised equipment.

'He's in intensive care,' Malik told them.

'Can we go in?'

'Not yet. The doctor's coming down.'

'Where is Leyla?'

'With him.'

They sat on the edge of their chairs in the waiting room. Tariq's knees throbbed. One of the fluorescent lights above them flickered unevenly, bothering his eyes.

The doctor was a small man with a turban. Dr Singh. He knew Malik and they shook hands and bowed elaborately.

'The crisis has passed. He is fine for now.' The doctor's dark liquid eyes glanced at Tariq. 'He had a clot. In his left lung.'

'Did you give him warfarin?' Malik asked.

Dr Singh nodded. 'The clot has been eliminated. But he has pneumonia. And all the other issues, of course.'

'Can we see him?' Zaida said.

'Not now.'

'Of course not,' Malik said loudly, 'he's had a *clot*. He's in intensive care.'

Dr Singh touched Malik's arm gently while he addressed Tariq's mother. 'His wife will stay with him tonight. Tomorrow is better. Come in tomorrow after ten o'clock.'

They drove home among the day's first commuters. The eastern sky was rimmed with red. No-one had said it. Not the doctor. Not his parents. But Tariq knew. The coughing. The clot. *The other issues*.

Why hadn't they let him visit?

IN the morning, Rahim had been moved to a double room on the third floor. The second bed was unoccupied. The room overlooked a wooded park and its window framed the swaying crowns of yellow-leaved cottonwoods. Rahim was flat on his back, eyes closed. His big head lay on the pillow like an offering, face mottled, hair damp, skin coarse and grainy. He had lost weight. An IV drip led to a catheter on his hand and thin tubes ran from an oxygen canister at the side of his bed, over his ears and into a clip in his nostrils.

When he opened his eyes and saw Tariq and his parents, he blinked and looked around as if he couldn't remember where he was. He removed the tubing from his nose.

'What are you doing?' Malik said.

'I only need it when I'm sleeping.'

His voice wheezed, even gurgled. His breathing was laboured, his eyes bloodshot and watery. Zaida kissed him on both cheeks, holding his head in her hands.

'Did you meet Leyla?' he said hoarsely. 'She just left. Went down for tea.'

'No.'

'She was with me all night. Took charge. Told the nurses what to do.' He smiled weakly, extended a scarred hand to Tariq. 'Rickey. Not in school?'

'You have pneumonia,' Malik said, as if delivering a diagnosis. 'What are you taking for the fever?'

'What am I *not* taking? They have me so full of drugs I can't remember what day it is.'

Zaida took Rahim's hand from Tariq's grasp and stroked it. 'Allah will look after you,' she said. 'You are strong and Allah is stronger.'

'Allah, maybe. Me, I'm not so sure.'

When he spoke, Rahim showed a spark of his usual fire. But the effort was intense and between responses his face was like a wet rag. Zaida talked for both of them, caressing his limp hand, her voice lively and hopeful. Like his father, Tariq stared, wondering how she knew what to say, the way to say it.

After ten minutes she laid his hand on the coverlet as if putting an injured bird back in its nest. She said she was going downstairs to find Leyla. Rahim told Malik to go with her. 'I want to talk to Rickey.'

Malik said he would stay. Rahim insisted. Malik lingered.

'Go, go,' Rahim said with what energy he had.

He coughed roughly, nodding at a chair beside the bed. Tariq sat. Neither said anything while Rahim recovered his breath. Outside, the treetops stirred in the wind, bright yellow against the slate-blue sky.

'In Baghdad they would say that your mother is a friend of Allah.'

'They didn't tell me how sick you are,' Tariq said.

'Why would they do that?'

'So I would come to see you.'

'Well, here you are. You're seeing me now.'

Suddenly, violently, Tariq sobbed. Rahim reached across and, with surprising strength, put his arm around Tariq's shoulder and drew him to his chest.

When Tariq had calmed down, Rahim whispered, 'It will take more than a blood clot to bring me down, Rickey. If those pigs in al-Jadriya couldn't break me, what makes you think pneumonia will?'

'It's just pneumonia?'

'Whatever it is, it doesn't frighten me. So don't let it frighten you.'

Tariq returned to the chair, wiped his eyes. The skin on his uncle's face was loose, the scars on his neck pale. 'I'm sorry,' Tariq said.

'You don't have to apologise. Did you bring your clarinet?'

'No. It's broken. A crack in the wood.'

'Cracks give character. You've seen my oud. Sing me a song.'

'I don't think so.'

'Sing "Forgive Me".'

'I don't remember it.'

'Of course you do.'

Rahim hummed the tune, and the roughness of his voice brought back the dust and noise of Baghdad, before the time of chaos and torture. Street musicians, beggars, the roar of passing trucks. Loudspeakers in the palm trees blaring political slogans. Old men playing chess in Abu Nuwas Park. Brown alleyways tangled with electricity wires and the muddy smell of the Tigris. Were these really his memories, or what his mother and Rahim had described to him? Did it matter?

Tariq sang over the broken tones of Rahim's fading voice. The Arabic words caressed his throat. Their literal meaning escaped him, but the music was stately, like an old riverboat moving slowly in the sunset.

When they finished, Rahim broke into a jagged cough that grew worse the more he tried to control it. His face reddened, his head flew forward, blood spattered the sheet. Alarmed, Tariq patted his back. Rahim shook him off. Tariq ran to the corridor and found a nurse, who calmed Rahim and fitted a full oxygen mask over his mouth. Above the mask, the blood-streaked eyes stared, wide and fearful.

The nurse, a young Filipino man with spiky hair, told Tariq to leave, that Rahim needed to rest. Rahim shook his head, made a sound and grabbed Tariq's arm.

'Looks like he wants you to stay,' the nurse said, smiling. 'See that button there? Any problem, you just press.'

His shoes squeaked across the polished floor as he left the room. Tariq clutched the seat of his chair, as dazed as if he'd been in a car crash. Slowly, Rahim recovered. A few minutes later, he took off the mask. 'Listen to an old man, Rickey. Never smoke. I smoked for thirty years and now look at me.'

His voice was grainy and gasping.

'Should I go and get Leyla?'

'No. Stay with me. They'll all be back soon enough.'

They stared at the rearing cottonwoods, the undersides of the leaves flashing in the wind and sun like bursts of fireworks. Above the trees, a tiny jet hung motionless, parallel contrails fading in its wake.

'Don't look so glum, Rickey. You are a young man. Girls and music, that's what you should be thinking about. Enjoying life.' He lifted a thin finger. 'But without smoking.'

Tariq longed for his mother, who could tell him what to say.

'Aren't you afraid?'

'No. What's to be afraid of? Pain? It could not be worse than what the Shia animals did to me. Paradise? How could I be afraid of paradise?'

'Do you believe in paradise?'

'What do you believe?'

'I don't believe what the imam tells us.'

Rahim smiled. 'What, no perfect garden? No eight doors? No ruby valleys? So what is there – nothing?'

'I don't know.'

Rahim leaned forward. His head hung like an old dog's. 'Let me tell you something, Rickey. You know as well as the imams do. Believe me. It is a mystery for us and a mystery for them.'

He turned his head to the window. Barely audibly, he said, 'I'll know before all of them. Or not.'

THAT night Tariq heard the drone of his parents' voices long after they had gone to bed. Zaida had driven them home from the hospital, Malik slumped against the car window, silent and still. The day had been long and listless. Malik went to work. Tariq busied himself as best he could: he bought a new phone, and was able to keep his old number. Spent several hours in the garage, fixing his bike. Zaida stayed in the kitchen, speaking several times with Leyla on the phone and cooking a white bean stew. The food was like ashes in Tariq's mouth. After eating he went to his room. He was still awake six hours later, when his father seemed to have found his voice. Perhaps he was praying.

Tariq did. He began with improvised sentiments but fell back on verses he had been taught: 'I ask Allah who is lofty and the Lord of the mighty Throne that he cure Ammu Rahim.' He repeated it seven times, as prescribed, remembering as he did the contradiction that always puzzled him: the prayer will enable the ill person to regain his health, unless he dies; when death is written it cannot be prevented.

How did that make sense?

And yet he prayed.

He woke in the middle of the night. His lamp was on and he was still in his clothes. He changed into his pyjamas and got under the covers. He couldn't sleep. He got up and retrieved his leather-bound notebook of poems from the bottom drawer of his desk.

Inside the front flap Rahim had written: *For Rickey – a place to keep the music of your heart.*

He leafed through the volume. Poems he had written about music, about his past, about Rachel. He came to his most recent. He stopped after reading the lines

in the rolling currents I see my death
it stares at me like a shining fish

He tore the page from the notebook, ripped it up and threw it in the waste basket.

Chapter 18

A BLACK SEDAN was parked across the street from Jamal's, exhaust puffing from the tailpipe, two men in suits and sunglasses in the front seat. Tariq arrived on his bike. As he locked it to the fence mesh he heard a whistle. The guy in the passenger seat motioned him over.

'You a friend of Jamal?'

'Yes.'

'Do me a favour.' He handed Tariq an envelope through the window. 'Give this to him.'

'Why don't you do it?'

The man grinned. His teeth were perfectly even and unnaturally white. 'Tell him hi, but we gotta run. We're making deliveries all over the place.'

The car eased away.

The blinds were down on all the windows and several free newspapers, wet and curling at the edges, lay on the porch. Tariq knocked. Nothing stirred. Again. As he was about to leave, the door cracked open, stopped abruptly by its security chain. Someone peered out.

'Jamal?'

'That you, Tariq?' he said.

He closed the door, undid the chain and opened it again. Pushed the screen wide with his knee but blocked the doorway as he checked the street.

'Where'd they go?'

'The guys in the car?'

'Motherfuckers.'

Tariq waited for Jamal to let him in. He didn't move.

Tariq held out the letter. 'They asked me to give you this.'

'Who did?'

'One of the men.'

Jamal snatched the envelope and flipped it into the muddy street. Bared his teeth. 'So they got you doing their dirty work, that it? All week acting like I don't exist and now you doing *their* bidding?'

His features were fierce and fixed, his African mask face. Bits of fluff clung to the underside of his beard.

'What do you mean?'

'Shit. Don't act dumb on me. Called you ten times. And you ignore my messages like those assholes in city hall.'

'I lost my phone, Jamal. I didn't get any messages.'

Jamal rattled the screen door with his shoulder. His eyes had the same wild cast they had the day he confronted Charmaine. 'That a fact? That why you just upped and disappeared on me?'

'I didn't. I tried to come here on Thursday. I crashed my bike and had to go home.'

Jamal stared at the bike, locked to the mesh fence. 'Bullshit. You're just like everyone else.'

He retreated, letting the screen door slam. Tariq grabbed its edge as it bounced off the frame and pushed himself through the entry so quickly and forcefully that he knocked Jamal back on his heels. Panic stung his throat like bile. Jamal bullying him. Of all people.

'My uncle is dying,' he shouted. 'In the Deaconess. He's dying from...'

He couldn't say the word. Through hot, blurry eyes he saw Jamal reach for him.

'Whoa, now. Take it easy. Don't start blubbering on me, now, you hear?'

He wrapped his arm around Tariq and held him close. He smelled as if he hadn't had a shower in a while. 'Be cool, my man,' he said. 'Be cool.'

When Tariq had calmed, Jamal stepped back. The living room was shaded and unlit and messier than ever. The air hot and stuffy. The stale smell of Jamal's clothes was in fact the odour of the whole house.

Tariq wiped his eyes.

'You want a soda or something?' Jamal said.

'No.'

Jamal gazed at the room as if noticing its squalor for the first time. 'Let's get out of here,' he said.

THEY took their usual walk along the railroad tracks. The sky was cloudless. Jamal wore wraparound sunglasses and an army field jacket with his unit patch and an American flag stitched to the shoulder sleeve. Along the way, kids on BMX bikes were trick-jumping the slopes of the railway embankment and ploughing through piles of dead leaves. Their shouts rode the clear air like train whistles.

This time Tariq did the talking. The words flowed like a prayer, effortless and incessant. He told Jamal scenes from family history: his grandfather, the archaeologist, who was fired without pension from the National Museum a year before retirement; the cousin who was arrested and never seen again; the flight from Baghdad; Rahim's refusal to leave until he was tortured. Details he didn't know he knew dropped into his narrative. Screams near the river. Killing scorpions in the alleyways. Watching his mother's brothers play dominoes at the tea house. He spoke of music: *maqam* and *choubi*, *bezikh* and *mawal*. Rahim's oud-playing and Leyla's poetry.

When he had talked himself out they walked in silence. They passed the fairground. Farm smells on the light wind. Empty animal stalls. The sadness of summer long gone. The shadow of grain elevators darkened the rutted fields.

They sat on a dusty hay bale, facing the sun. Jamal said, 'You keep playing his music, man. His tunes. Your *country's* tunes.'

Tariq's clarinet lay in five broken pieces under his bed. He had no urge to bring it in for repair. After singing 'Forgive Me' with Rahim, playing or even listening to any other music was empty.

'You back with the high-school band?'

Tariq answered without thinking. 'I'm not even back in high school. My father enrolled me in the mosque.'

Jamal sat upright and took off his sunglasses. 'He did *what*? When did this happen?'

Tariq grasped a handful of hay from between his legs. 'Well, it's not final. It's, like, if I don't get back into Monroe High, I go there.'

'And why wouldn't you get back in?'

Tariq threw the hay in the air and the breeze blew the stalks back in his face. He sneezed. 'Let's leave that one for today, Jamal, OK?'

'You want to *leave* it?'

'That's what I said.'

Jamal tilted his head and creased his eyes, chewed an earpiece of his sunglasses.

'*What?*' Tariq said.

Jamal raised his hand. 'Hey, I ain't said nothing.'

The shadows stretched in front of them. A dog raced across the open field, dead leaves spiralling in its wake. From the elevator docks came the sound of a grain truck grinding its gears.

'How come you haven't opened the store yet?' Tariq said.

Jamal spat heavily onto the dirt. 'Bank's trying to foreclose on me.'

'What does that mean?'

'It means I ain't made my mortgage payments. But how can I do that when the city won't renew my retail permit? You tell me how I'm going to make any money when I can't sell any records.'

'Why don't you just get the permit?'

Jamal sprang to his feet. 'I will not pay no goddamn taxes. Where you been the last month. I *told* you. You pay taxes to an immoral government, then you immoral yourself. Is that so hard to understand?'

'Well, maybe if you told them –'

'What the fuck do you know about it? I told you, man. Nobody *listens*.'

He shook his head at the sky and strode off.

Tariq followed at a distance. After a while, Jamal looked over his shoulder. He waited for Tariq to catch up. They walked side by side.

'I guess we both got topics we don't want to talk about.'

'Yeah. I guess.'

They followed the railroad tracks to the sand and gravel pit and then took a shortcut past the old quarry. As they skirted the quarry pond, Tariq heard a shout, clear as the crack of a baseball bat: 'Hey, freak!'

He knew the voice at once. He didn't look.

'You. I'm talking to *you*, asshole.'

Jamal stopped.

'Keep going,' Tariq said.

'Keep *going*? Hang on a minute.'

Though he dared not look directly, he knew three of them were there. They sat at the base of the quarry wall, on a shelf of weathered stone popular in the summer with swimmers and sunbathers. Behind them, unleaved willow branches hung above the pond like whips. The still, glassy water reflected the mossy jut of the wall and the deep blue of the sky.

'You know those guys?'

Tariq stared at the water, saying nothing.

'They them motherfuckers you told me about?'

'Can we just go home, Jamal?'

'We ain't going nowhere.'

Jamal started down the trail to the pond, wading through buckthorn and canary grass. Terrified to follow, terrified not to, Tariq moved after him a few steps at a time. One of the kids stood up. Tariq didn't recognise him. Brad stayed where he was, supine in the sun, hands laced behind his head. In spite of the cold weather he wore a sleeveless T-shirt. His boots were off and sat on a rock above his head. The third person was a girl, also unfamiliar. She was young, with stringy strawberry blond hair and a blank face. She sat hunched beside Brad, holding his baseball cap and squinting at Jamal.

An arm of the pond lay between the curve of the trail and the spot where the kids were grouped. Getting to them meant circling the inlet, so Jamal stopped and faced them across about twenty feet of water.

'You say something?'

'Not to you I didn't,' Brad said, shading his eyes with his palm.

Jamal stepped to his right, inviting Tariq to stand beside him. Tariq felt the warmth of the sun on his neck, the cool air off the water before him. The hum of fear in his stomach.

'You talk trash to my buddy here,' Jamal said, 'you talk trash to me.'

'Is that right?'

'That's right.'

Brad got to his feet. He took his cap from the girl and put it on with the brim angled high. His sneer was so pronounced he looked like a cartoon character. 'So what is this – your chickenshit little buddy can't fight his own battles? Can't even open his mouth, it looks like.'

Jamal reached into the grass beside his leg, snapped off a stalk and stuck it in his mouth. Tariq could hear him exhaling abruptly from his nostrils, like a bull.

'We're just hanging out, mister,' Brad said.

'Hanging out insulting folks.'

'Nothing to do with you. Mohammad there has some history with me. Some history with the nation. Or do you have no idea what people like him want to do to people like us?'

He pointed a thumb at the kid beside him. The boy smirked. He was big, with cow eyes and a face darkened by a narrow life. He stared intently across the water, but Tariq was not as scared as he'd expected.

'Apologise to my man here,' Jamal said.

Brad laughed. 'Do *what*?'

The other boy picked up a heavy rock and threw it across the divide so that it splashed in front of Jamal and wet his pants legs.

'They might call you psycho,' the kid said, 'but you don't scare us.'

'Hey, freak,' Brad said, pointing at Tariq. 'Fuck you *and* your psycho cripple friend.'

Like a wolf, Jamal loped around the inlet in huge athletic strides. The girl screamed. Brad jumped off the rock and stubbed his toe.

He leapt about in pain. By the time Jamal reached them, the other kid had stepped in front of Brad. Jamal punched him in the neck and he fell in the weeds like a roped calf. Brad limped forward, crouched like a boxer, fists raised. Jamal kicked him between the legs and grabbed him by the hair and dragged him out away from the rockface. The other boy was rolling in the dirt, clutching his neck and groaning. The girl let loose a torrent of swear words that echoed in the quarry.

Jamal got Brad onto all fours, facing the water. He still had Brad by the hair, so that his face was thrust forward, savage and distended. Jamal's knee was in his back. There was a flurry of garbled words between them, but Tariq understood nothing. Then Jamal let go of Brad's hair and kicked him hard in the ass so that he plunged into the water.

The girl was yelling that Brad couldn't swim, but the water was only three feet deep and he flailed and swore and got to his feet. Calmly, Jamal walked around the inlet, his face without expression, and headed back the way they had come. Tariq followed. Behind them, Brad's swearing continued.

Chapter 19

RAHIM died on Sunday night. Leyla was with him. Malik was en route from Monroe General, where he had been working the night shift. He drove quickly through the quiet streets but had no chance of arriving before the end. Within ten minutes of Dr Singh's call, Rahim was gone.

Tariq found out when he came down for breakfast on Monday morning. His father sat at the kitchen table, rocking back and forth. His mother stood behind him, hands on his shoulders. They looked exhausted, squeezed dry of all passion, though they had clearly been crying for a while.

Brave-faced, Zaida embraced Tariq and whispered the news. Her arms clutched him protectively, but he felt worse for his parents than for himself. He sat beside his father and touched his hand. Malik stared at him blankly, then rubbed his head with his fingertips. On the tabletop was a litter of tea glasses, spoons and crumpled tissues. His father's folded reading glasses. A bit of orange peel. Grains of sugar scattered like sand on the floor of a tent.

'When I got to the Deaconess,' Malik said, 'I couldn't find a parking space. It was terrible. I nearly crashed into the fence I was so upset. I went directly to his room. Didn't even stop at reception. Where his bed had been there was an empty space. I can still see it. This *absence*. In the other bed was an old man, asleep. Much older than Rahim.'

He spoke as if Tariq had been sitting beside him for hours. His voice was thin and wavering, like a candle flame. While he talked, Zaida remained standing, swaying gently from side to side.

'Leyla was nowhere to be found. There seemed to be some sort of crisis – voices over the intercom, people rushing about. Or maybe it was me. My own panic. In any case it took me several minutes to find a nurse who knew who Rahim was. She told me to follow her. As we walked down the hall she said, "You were told that he was ill, weren't you?" The stupid woman! So at that moment I knew he had passed away. We went to the end of the hallway and the nurse opened a door and there was Leyla – poor Leyla – sitting on a plastic chair. A red plastic chair in a room so small it could have been a closet. Someone had given her a cup of tea in a Styrofoam cup and she had spilled the tea and broken the cup into tiny pieces.

'I can't remember what she said. I just have this picture of her in my mind, framed in the doorway, staring up at me, saying nothing. Like a drawing in an old manuscript. Such sorrow! And I was struck dumb too. Stood there, like a tree. But inside of me… Eventually we prayed, of course, she and I, and after a few minutes Dr Singh arrived and told us we could view Rahim's body. He was in a room beside us. The whole time! Even though the doctor is a Sikh he was aware of our customs and Rah's eyes had been closed and his body… his body…'

He broke down. His head fell and his pointed shoulders shuddered. Zaida went to him, but he pushed away her hands and stood and waved his arms and said fiercely, 'Don't you see? I am his *brother*.'

LATER that day Tariq and his father drove to Lonergan's Funeral Home in Verona. Malik had calmed but said nothing on the ride. Imam Mohammad met them at the entrance. He and Malik spoke quietly. The imam had stepped in as soon as Malik had called him, contacting the mosque's religious affairs committee, arranging for the body to be moved from the hospital, filling out forms and paying fees. In spite of the Irish name, the home had staff who understood Islamic requirements. Its representative, a bearded man dressed in a dark suit, stood off to the side, hands folded at his belt, waiting for the imam to introduce him. Head bowed, he whispered condolences in perfect Arabic.

The man led them to a hushed reception area, where Malik signed some forms, and then to a large tiled room at the rear of the building. The cold room was high-ceilinged and windowless. Long strips of fluorescent lighting gave it a blue glow. Along the walls folding screens were set up at intervals, and behind one of the screens, Rahim's body lay on a long metal shelf. The shelf had raised edges and a drain in the corner. Beside it was a sink and a cabinet with stainless steel bowls, washcloths and towels. The corpse was covered from the neck down with a sheet.

Tariq's heart thumped and his head grew light. He had failed to imagine the impact of this moment. He was shocked. It wasn't that Rahim's face, eyes closed, mouth slightly agape, looked much different. It was that he *wasn't there*. Whatever had defined him was gone and what was left was pale and rubbery and cold.

It was the responsibility of male members of the family to bathe the body. Tariq knew this. He steeled himself for the task. While they prepared the ablutions, the undertaker removed the sheet and Rahim's hospital clothing and covered the genitals with a loose cloth. Tariq averted his eyes. Ensuring that Rahim's face was towards Mecca, the imam recited from the Qur'an. After prayer, he unrolled a piece of muslin and spread it over the body.

Following his father's lead, Tariq filled his bowl with scented water and poured it slowly on the cloth. They repeated this action until the whole cloth was soaked. Malik gathered the cloth in folds, gently rubbing the corpse with its corners. They washed the body three times, always with fresh towels, beginning on the right side. The hair on Rahim's chest was thick and matted. The scars on his hands and neck had turned from pink to purple. His injured leg was withered beneath the knee. Malik cleaned the private areas, a washcloth wrapped around his hand. When they were finished, they patted him dry and the imam perfumed the body with rose oil and camphor.

The funeral representative wheeled in a cart holding the shroud, wrapped in brown paper. The imam unwrapped it and laid out the required three pieces of linen. They were brilliantly white and soft and smelled like flowers. More prayers, and then, with the greatest tenderness and respect, Tariq and Malik wrapped Rahim's remains in this fragrant covering, taking care to fold and tuck exactly as the imam directed, leaving the face exposed. When they were finished, the imam arranged the cloth around the face like the corolla of a flower. He stepped away. The coldness was gone. Ammu Rahim looked at peace.

The representative left them and the imam recited the final *da'awat*. The Arabic rose from their small circle like smoke from a campfire, swirling and echoing in the frigid room. Malik sniffled as he responded. His hands shook. Rahim lay before them like a martyr. Under his breath, Tariq hummed 'Forgive Me'. The melody and the drone of the prayer cleared his head and beneath the sting of rising tears he felt a lightness in his limbs and a lifting in his heart.

THE funeral was held the next day, in accordance with sharia law. The male mourners gathered in the square outside Masjid

As-Sunnah in brilliant sun, shoes off, to say *salat al-Janazah*. Many were dressed in traditional cloaks and skullcaps, including Tariq and his father. They formed three long rows, with the imam out front, facing Mecca. He stood near the head of Rahim's enshrouded body, which lay on an open wooden platform enclosed by slatted rails. It had been wrapped in a navy blue blanket embroidered with gold thread, which Zaida had brought from Baghdad. Tariq's grandmother had given it to her the day of her marriage, twenty years ago. For as long as Tariq could remember, the blanket had hung on the back wall of his parents' room, above their bed.

Leyla had stayed with the Mussams the night before. Zaida had gone with her from the hospital to her house, where they collected Rahim's oud, selections from his CD collection and his photograph in a silver frame. Leyla wore a plain black hijab and a grey cloak. She wore no make-up or jewellery and her pale face looked ravaged. Every time she saw Tariq she started crying.

Women from the mosque arrived with food and flowers, and Zaida played selections from the CDs as well as Iraqi religious music. The men sat in the kitchen, drinking mint tea and telling stories about Baghdad before the war. Amir Rahman, who had been a bookseller on Mutanabbi Street, read the passage from the *Epic of Gilgamesh* in which the king grieves for his friend Enkidu and roams the wild landscape clothed in animal skins. Malik talked about Rahim as a boy. As the hours passed, the reminiscing grew more sentimental and Malik had to leave the room several times.

After the visitors had left, Tariq's mother and Leyla stayed in the living room, talking and praying. Tariq, who couldn't sleep, heard their voices until five in the morning, when Zaida convinced Leyla to rest for a few hours before the funeral.

In spite of clear skies, the day was very cold and windy, and the flagstones of the mosque square chilled the mourners' stocking feet. Yusef and his father were there and many of the men who had been to the football match. Mahmoud Khan stood beside Malik. Every few minutes, he discreetly grasped his friend's elbow. His son was beside Tariq. After the silent prayers, the imam led the congregation though the *dua* for the prophet and the supplication to Allah for the deceased. *Assalamu wlaikum warahmatullah*, the imam intoned, his voice ringing in the cold air.

Tariq heard himself respond, 'O God, if he was a doer of good, then increase his good deeds, and if he was a wrongdoer, then overlook his bad deeds.' He did not ever remember having learned the prayer. *Allahu akbar*, he said, and repeated the phrase seven times.

After the service, a cortege of cars followed the hearse to Highland cemetery. Because of the cemetery's distance from the mosque, the requirement to walk behind the coffin had been lifted. Tariq sat beside his father in the black Lincoln limousine. Malik stared at the sombre streets, dulled by the tinted windows. Leyla cried silently, leaning on Zaida's shoulder. Whether by design or not – Tariq didn't know – the cortege passed the garage where Rahim had been working as a mechanic. It had been closed for the day as a mark of respect.

They arrived at Highland and slowly made their way to the Muslim section at the rear of the cemetery, a grassy rise surrounded by a wrought-iron fence and shaded by poplars and laurels. The section was new, purchased four years ago by the religious affairs committee, with only a scattering of graves. Rahim's burial plot was in the far corner, where dead leaves shepherded by the wind had gathered against the fence and the branches of bare trees glistened in the sun. The mourners filed in, forming a semicircle. The women stood to one side.

Tariq had not been to a burial that he could remember. But the details were inexplicably familiar. The grave had been dug so that it was perpendicular to the *Qibla*. Mounds of fresh dirt rose on both sides of a temporary wooden marker. A simple wreath lay at the foot of the opening like a lifebuoy.

After the drama of the previous twenty-four hours, the last act was swift. The imam, voice hoarse, led the final prayers. The wind lifted, and the wings of the women's scarves and the folds of their cloaks swirled and flapped. At the imam's cue, Malik propped Rahim's head and shoulders with three balls of soil, so that he would face to the right, and to Mecca, for eternity. Before the body was lowered, the mourners passed the grave, each throwing in three handfuls of earth, except for Leyla, who threw in a rose and a written piece of music, which fluttered onto the body like a butterfly.

As the gravediggers lifted their shovels, Tariq turned away. In the distance, a hot air balloon, striped red and yellow against brilliant blue, drifted silently above the windswept lake.

Chapter 20

THANKSGIVING. In recent years the Mussams had celebrated quietly, if only by having Rahim and Leyla over for dinner. After all, school was out, businesses were shut, Malik was rarely on call. Zaida arranged it. Once she had even cooked a turkey. Tariq's father did not approve. Muslims give thanks to Allah every day of the year, he said, so why would we mark a holiday for it? But she liked to prepare *kibbe batata*, brew tea and gossip with Leyla as her husband wandered in and out of the kitchen, grumbling. And Tariq enjoyed listening to Rahim play Iraqi ballads on his oud while the muted television danced with the slash and colour of college football.

But this year the holiday was only a week after Rahim's funeral. The day passed without mention. That week it had snowed – only an inch or two, but enough to smother any last hopes of an Indian summer. The city was scuffed and coarse. Clouds like steel wool pressed close to the tired hills and the wind turned bitter. On neighbouring porch-fronts the hanging garlands of wheat and corn suggested not harvest but loss.

Against the wishes of the imam, Leyla had stayed with Tariq's family after the funeral, though she did not leave the house for three days. She wore the same hijab and cloak and cried continually. For hours at a time she sat on the living room sofa, Rahim's framed photograph in her hands. Zaida cancelled her classes and stayed home, cooking, telling stories, holding Leyla's hand when grief overwhelmed her. Though Tariq helped his mother and aunt, running errands and doing small jobs around the house, most of the time he stayed in his room, nervous and desperate.

His father worked long hours at the hospital. At home he refused food, claiming he was eating at work, but day by day he grew more gaunt, with plum-coloured bags beneath his eyes and deep lines that ran from the corners of his mouth to the base of his chin. Tariq was no longer afraid: his father looked as if he hadn't the strength to raise his arm, never mind hit him. On the fourth day, when Leyla changed back into Western clothes and stopped weeping, Malik came home from the hospital mid-afternoon, went straight to his bedroom and did not appear for the rest of the day. Late that night, Tariq, unable himself to sleep, heard him pacing the floors downstairs. Once, he heard a sharp cry, cut short, followed by a deep sob.

His father's withdrawal made Tariq feel even more bereft. The house was like a crypt, his bedroom like a coffin. He would wake from troubled sleep gasping for breath, the sheets soaked. During the day he busied himself, collecting dry cleaning or buying groceries for his mother, browsing in the music store, bringing his clarinet in for repair, even checking Starbucks in case Rachel might be there. But the flutter of despair in his chest would not cease, and the weight of circumstance pressed against him like cold earth. When he found Jamal's shop still locked up, dusty and derelict, loneliness blew through him. Who was left for him? Who could protect him?

His parents passed through a grief shaped by their age and past. He grieved as well, but the spin of his sadness was different. Rahim had told him to enjoy life. Five weeks out of school, he was more conscious than ever of a new world floating into the future without him. On Wednesday, as he swept light snow from the front sidewalk, he stopped mid-movement, checked his watch, and realised that the school band was in the middle of the Thanksgiving concert. His bandmates and their families would all be in the gym. Mr Broquist would be waving the baton, glasses at the end of his nose. For all he knew, at that very moment Josh Hall was playing the Gershwin *glissando*, while Rachel listened, rapt, from the wooden seats.

Jamal had fallen silent. He did not answer his phone or return messages. Twice Tariq had cycled to his house and knocked repeatedly, but glimpsed no signs of life. He considered walking around the house and peering through the back windows but stopped short when he remembered the cabinet full of guns.

They had not met since the confrontation with Brad at the quarry. At first Tariq had relished the sense of vengeance. But he soon saw that Brad's humiliation had made the situation worse. How could he return to Monroe High now? He was looking over his shoulder every time he left the house. And with al-Hijra beginning at the end of November, he was a month away from the Islamic new year and the start of mosque school. *You'll end up listening to the imam all day*, Rahim had said. *Is that what you want?*

ON Saturday afternoon Tariq got a text from an unknown number: *my store is trashed, can u help me clean up – J.*

He called Jamal but it went straight to voicemail. He cycled to Hawthorne Row, taking care on the icy streets. Shoppers crowded the roads, on their way to the malls for the Thanksgiving sales, but most of the small businesses downtown were closed. Tariq locked his bike against a lamp-post. In the holiday quiet he heard the hum of distant traffic and the clink of a halyard on an empty flagpole. The millrace had begun to freeze, and ice sheathed a foot or two of the canal's edges with the thinnest of panes.

The steps down to the shop's basement entrance were cluttered with plastic bottles and old newspaper. Lying on the gritted concrete apron in front of the shop door were several record sleeves, muddy and torn and stained with the chevroned prints of heavy boots. The door was ajar.

Inside, the place was a mess. As Tariq's eyes adjusted to the gloom, he saw record bins overturned, posters torn from the walls, shattered vinyl littering the aisles. Exposed wiring hung from the low ceiling. A light was on at the rear. In its dull glow Tariq saw that the front panels of the service counter were sprayed with red paint, the mirror behind the cash register cracked.

'Jamal,' he shouted. 'It's me.'

He moved down the aisle. There was a bad smell, a sewer smell. He righted a few of the bins and replaced some records. Someone came out from behind the counter.

It was Brad.

Tariq turned away. Brad's friend, the kid from the quarry, stood at the entrance, arms folded across his chest. Tariq stepped sideways, knocking over one of the damaged bins. He found it hard to breathe. It was as if he'd been locked in the trunk of a car.

'Not who you were looking for?' Brad said.

The two boys moved slowly down the aisle. Slipping on discarded record sleeves, Tariq scrambled through the debris, backing up until he was against the wall. He took his phone from his pocket. Moving quickly, Brad snatched it and flung it across the store. In the same motion he removed his baseball cap and, holding it by the bill, slapped Tariq across the face. The plastic adjuster caught the wing of Tariq's nose. It stung sharply, and when he touched his face he felt blood.

'Oh, yeah,' Brad said. 'Big man now. Big man without your psycho ghetto protector.'

'He's not my protector.'

'So why'd you send him after us?'

'I told him not to.'

Brad laughed and spat in Tariq's face.

'Right. Like you didn't enjoy watching. And for your information, he fights dirty. Rabbit-punches Ronny and pulls my hair. I didn't even have my boots on. Pushes me from behind like a girl. Then runs away. That is *such* bullshit.'

Tariq watched Ronny. He had picked up an eighteen-inch length of wood and was holding it like a club.

'I'm with my friends, minding my own business, and you come along with the fucking sickest dude in town. Everyone *knows* what he's like.'

'Shoulda pressed charges,' Ronny said.

'Wouldn't give that piece of shit the satisfaction.'

'You threw that rock,' Tariq said. 'You called him names.'

Brad pressed close. 'Names? How about "infidel"? "American pigs"? You Muslims *invented* name-calling.'

'I've never called you anything.'

Brad punched Tariq in the stomach. His whole body collapsed in on itself. He couldn't breathe. He clutched at his gut and fell forward so that his head bumped against Brad's chest. Brad shoved him back, hard, and his head bounced off the wall. Desperately, he gulped air. His hearing faded in and out. Brad was shouting and punching. Ronny yelled and shook the piece of wood. Then, as when he found himself suddenly awake at the darkest point of night, Tariq's mind was sharp and empty. And into this vacuum anger rushed like a drug.

He threw himself at Brad, who tripped and fell with Tariq on top of him. He clawed and grabbed and clutched him by the throat. He was crying and shouting in Arabic and raking Brad's face with

178

his nails and trying to slam his head off the floor. Everything was a blur. He felt blows on his head and back but no pain. He flailed and pounded, drowning in the salt-and-metal taste of his rage. Then, as quickly as he had lost his temper, all faded.

When he came to, he was lying face down in blood and dust. The world resurfaced like a radio being tuned. An awful throb and a high ringing in his ears. His left cheek felt twice its size. For a moment he remembered nothing. He propped himself on an elbow and touched his face. It was sticky with blood. He could not see out of his left eye.

The boys were gone. Tariq got to his feet, dizzy and nauseated. He groped his way to the front door and sat on the outside steps. The cold air felt good, but his head still pounded. He allowed his stomach to settle and went back inside to look at himself in the cracked mirror. He had expected his face to be swollen and grotesque, but apart from a scrape below his eye and streaks of blood from his nose, he didn't look much different. But his coat was torn and bloodstained and he had lost most of his shirt buttons.

The cash register had been upended and pulled to the floor. Tariq passed through the bead curtain at the back and found a bathroom. He used the toilet and washed the blood from his face. His hands were steady. Sight had returned to his eye, but his cheek hurt like hell and his head throbbed. He was empty of emotion, and not even the thought that Brad and Ronny might be waiting for him on the street worried him. He looked for his phone but couldn't find it. In a corner he found the source of the bad smell – a mound of shit, still steaming in the cold. His stomach lurched again and he left the store. On his way out he found a John Coltrane record sleeve, ripped in half.

Someone needed to tell Jamal.

The street was deserted. He could not remember the combination to his bike lock. He sat on the kerb, head in his hands. What would he do? Walk home? Where else could he go? He stared at the gutter. Black birds squawked overhead. Flecks of snow danced in the air. He would phone Jamal. No, he would go to his house. He would get a cab.

He got up, grew dizzy, slumped to the ground on his hands and knees.

'Hey, you OK?'

Russell, Jamal's friend from the coffee shop, leaned over him, dreadlocks hanging like a curtain from beneath the knitwork of his Jamaican cap. His small face was like a rosebud, rolled tight with concern.

He helped Tariq to his feet. 'I have to go to Jamal's,' Tariq said.

'You're not going anywhere, buddy. Come with me.'

Russell helped him into the coffee shop and made him a cup of tea. There were no other customers. Delicately, he tilted Tariq's head back, examining his wounds and peering into his eyes.

'You hit your head or what?'

'I got in a fight.'

'No shit.'

'Someone broke into the record store. Wrecked everything. I have to tell Jamal.'

Russell leaned back, his mouth pursed. Went to the window and looked down the street.

'This have anything to do with the kid you were fighting?' Russell said.

'Kids. There were two of them.'

'They did the store?'

'I don't know. Probably. They have it in for me. For Jamal too.'

Russell stood in front of the window, hands on his hips.

'Maybe we should call the police,' Tariq said. 'The door is still open over there.'

'You best leave that situation to me. Jamal, he isn't in the most righteous place right now. And definitely no *po*lice.'

'What about the store?'

Russell loosened his apron. 'Forget about the store. We need to get you patched up. I'll drive you to the hospital. Could be you're concussed. Could be you need stitches.'

'No hospital,' Tariq said sharply.

Russell shook his head. 'You need attention, son.'

'OK. So bring me home.'

Chapter 21

SLUMPED LOW in Russell's aging car, Tariq counted the passing telephone poles in time with the throbbing in his head. The familiar streets unravelled in short, vivid reels: schoolkids throwing handfuls of dead leaves; a squat postal truck trawling the kerb, steering wheel on the wrong side; Canada geese tearing blades of grass from the field beside the old train depot.

'You OK, son?'

'Kind of dizzy.'

'You hang in there. I'll get you home.'

Tariq couldn't find his key and Russell rang the bell. They heard the tap of his mother's shoes across the hall floor. The pause as she donned her hijab. When she opened the door and saw him, she stepped back and lifted a hand to her mouth. She made a sound he had not heard since he was a small boy in Baghdad. Like a frightened animal.

'Oh, *habibi*, who did this to you?' she said in Arabic.

She held him close. The feel of her soft clothes and the smell of her perfume caught him off guard. His throat and eyes burned. *I'm getting blood all over her good robe,* he thought, but he was limp in her arms and could do nothing but let her lead him to the living room, where she crouched before him and touched his face and hair and hands and spoke rapidly in Arabic, phrases he could not follow.

'It's not as bad as it looks,' he croaked.

But now that he was home he felt worse. His head and shoulders ached. The cuts on his face stung. He said he wanted to lie down.

'Not a good idea,' Russell said.

Zaida stared up at Russell, as if only just noticing him. The dreadlocks. The gaudy hat. The funky jacket and two-toned shoes.

'Ma'am, he could be concussed. Best you keep him alert until a doctor can check him out.'

She looked at Tariq's face and then back to Russell, bemused. 'You're Tariq's friend,' she said.

'You might be thinking of Jamal.'

'The disabled man.'

'He's not going to pitch for the Cubs any time soon, if that's what you mean.'

She rose to standing height, a hand on Tariq's shoulder. A lock of hair poked from beneath the hijab and curved across her brow like a comma. A bloodstain the size of a dollar coin marked her silk robe. 'What happened? Was this *another* crash? What did I tell you about that bike? About wearing a helmet?'

'It wasn't a bike crash,' Russell said.

'So what was it?'

Rubbing his chin, Russell glanced at Tariq. 'He's somewhat banged up, all right. But he wouldn't let me bring him to the hospital.'

'His father's a doctor.'

'Well, that's good to hear.'

'And I need to call him.' She had recovered her composure. Her gaze displayed gratitude for Russell's help but also wariness. 'Mr...?'

'Johnson, ma'am, Russell Johnson.'

'Mr Johnson. Thank you for looking after my son. Will you watch him for a minute more while I telephone?'

She phoned from the kitchen. Her voice was hushed and urgent. Russell sat with his arm around Tariq's sore shoulders.

'You're in good hands now.'

'I guess.'

'Your dad will take care of you. Lucky guy. A doctor in the house.'

The world was settling back into its accustomed shape. In the ornate Semitic tone of the Mussam living room, Tariq grew conscious of his family's old-world views. Where someone dressed like Russell would be seen as a beggar or a thief. The musty dreadlocks. The missing tooth. Soon his father would be home. He would want to know what had happened.

As soon as she was off the phone Zaida thanked Russell again and ushered him to the door. He smiled at Tariq as he left.

'Call Jamal,' Tariq said.

'Don't you worry about Jamal.'

'Thank you.'

Russell's car clanked away. Pain passed through Tariq's head in waves.

'What's the matter?'

'If I can't lie down I'll take a shower.'

'Oh, no, you won't. You will wait for your father so he can examine you.'

'Examine me?'

'Are you going to tell me what happened?'

Tariq didn't answer. Frowning, his mother pinched the fabric of her robe and pulled it away from her skin so that the bloodstain shone blackly in the overhead light.

He sat at the kitchen table while she cleaned his wounds. She had changed into a plainer robe and white hijab. The front door slammed and his father walked in, wan and on edge. Still in his overcoat, he peered into his son's eyes. Asked if he had been hit on the head, lost his sense of balance, had blurred vision or nausea. Where he was born. What day it was. He took pen and paper from his pocket and drew lines of numbers, connected by lines and arrows. He asked Tariq to read the numbers, in the order indicated by the arrows, as quickly as he could. He timed the responses.

'He is not concussed,' he said to Zaida, removing his coat.

'Does that mean I can lie down?' Tariq said.

Malik ignored him. He handed the coat to Zaida. The taut concern of his arrival had relaxed into a grey disdain. He washed his hands at the kitchen sink and held them in the air, like a surgeon preparing for an operation.

With wet fingers he pressed the swelling beneath Tariq's eye.

'Ow! That *hurts*.'

'It may hurt, but it is not broken.'

He parted the hair on the crown of Tariq's head.

'You'll need stitches here. And here.'

'Be careful, Malik. He is hurt.'

Again he washed his hands. 'You have him spoiled,' he said, his back to her. 'He's not a child any more.'

He dried his hands, grimacing. 'Get your coat,' he said to Tariq.

'Why?'

'You can't be stitched up here.'

SINCE his brother's death, Malik had hardly spoken to Tariq. He kept more and more to himself, staying in his bedroom, eating little, passing quickly from the house. And he had become even more religious. As well as observing *salat* five times a day, he murmured constantly, his worn prayer beads passing through his fingers like an ammunition belt. Zaida was careful what she said to him. And Tariq, though thankful that the shouting and threats had stopped, was also wary. Pity for his father's loss had given way to a sense that suffering and self-denial were coiling inside him like a snake.

They drove to the hospital in silence. Eventually his father asked him what had happened. Tariq had had time to consider his story.

'I fell down a flight of stairs.'

Malik stared at the road ahead, expressionless.

'Concrete stairs,' Tariq said. 'At my friend's record store on Hawthorne. It's one of those basement stores, and I went there because someone had broken in, and there were old record sleeves on the ground and I slipped on them. Slipped and fell.'

His father glanced at Zaida, who sat in the back seat. 'Is this what he told you?'

'He didn't tell me anything.'

'You have a friend who owns a store,' Malik said. 'A store on Hawthorne Row.'

'He is the disabled man,' Zaida said. 'Tariq has been helping him. It is part of his *zakat*.'

'He's giving this man *money*?'

'No. Time and help. As the imam directs.'

'So you were injured in a fall.'

'Yes,' Tariq said.

'You swear by Allah?'

Tariq grunted.

They drove not to Monroe General, where Malik worked, but to the Deaconess, where Rahim had died. They waited for a half an hour in the emergency room, amid pallid young men with broken limbs and old women who couldn't stay awake. Zaida brought him tea. His father kept his distance, pacing the floor, arms crossed, face ashen in the fluorescent light.

After Tariq had been stitched up and they had returned to the car, his father stared through the windshield for a long time, both hands on the wheel. Tariq closed his eyes and leaned against the headrest. All he wanted was to go home and lie down.

His father headed off in the opposite direction.

'What are you doing?' Zaida said. He didn't answer. 'Malik. Where are we going?'

He drove to the police station. As they pulled up, Zaida objected. He told her to be quiet and said to Tariq, 'Come with me.'

'Why?'

'Do you take me for a fool?'

'No.'

'I am a doctor. I work in the emergency room of a hospital.' He bared his teeth. 'Do you think I don't know when I've seen someone who has been beaten?'

'I fell.'

'Who did this to you?'

'No-one.'

Malik bit his lip and rubbed his unshaven chin with his fingers. 'Let's go.'

'I'll stay with Ommi.'

'Do you want the police to conduct their business out here? On the street?'

'What business?'

'Malik, this is silly. He needs to go home. He needs rest.'

'I will *not* be contradicted,' Malik screeched, thumping the wheel with his palm. 'I will not be questioned every day of my life. *Do you understand?* Both of you.'

The words bounced around the overheated confines of the car. Spittle flew from his mouth. His mother turned her face away, as if slapped.

'Go, Tariq. Go with Baba.'

'No.'

Malik got out of the car, opened the back door and tried to drag him from the rear seat. Tariq resisted and his father slipped on the slick pavement and cried out. A man walking his dog stopped and asked if everything was all right. Zaida spoke under her breath in Arabic. Tariq got out of the car and helped his father to his feet.

'He's fine,' Tariq said and followed Malik to the station door. Nothing could be worse than the scenario on the sidewalk. Behind them, his mother spoke rapidly to the man, and her laughter was as empty as the ring of a cell phone.

The station house was decorated for Thanksgiving, crepe bunting in orange and gold, baskets of Indian corn and multicoloured gourds. The reception area was as quiet as the holiday streets. A policeman sat at the receiving desk, the sports pages spread in front of him. In the corner were two other cops, out of uniform, watching a football game on television.

'Gentlemen, can I help you?' the first cop said, peering over the crescent lenses of his reading glasses.

'We wish to report an assault,' Malik said in a high-pitched voice.

One of the men at the TV peered over his shoulder, then returned his attention to the game. *No police*, Russell had said. The receiving cop slowly folded the newspaper and rose from his chair. He retrieved a pen and clipboard and came to the counter.

'Is everyone OK?' he said, looking at the cuts on Tariq's face.

'We have come directly from the hospital. My son has had to have ten stitches.'

His father's accent sounded dense and alien. He pointed at the wounds and Tariq leaned away from him.

'Is that right, son?'

'I got stitches, yeah.'

'From an assault?'

'Not exactly.'

The cop took off his glasses. His badge had a dent in it and his name tag said BARATELLI. He tapped the pen on the clipboard then and invited them to come inside the reception counter and sit at his desk.

'OK, gentlemen. Let's take this one step at a time. Your name, sir?'

'Mussam. Malik Mussam.'

'And the young man's name?'

Tariq spelled his name.

'So, Tariq, why don't you describe for me what happened.'

'He was attacked,' his father said, 'you can see that for yourself.'

'Mr Mussam –'

'*Dr* Mussam.'

'Dr Mussam, I need to hear it from the victim.'

'Tell him,' Malik said in Arabic. 'And if you lie you are committing a crime. Remember that.'

The cop did not register the change of language. He waited, his face broad and sympathetic.

'My father is mistaken. I wasn't attacked.'

Malik made a small noise.

The cop nodded. 'So what happened?'

'I got in a fight.'

The cop took in the bandage on Tariq's head, his swollen face. 'Tariq, anything you say in here is confidential, you know that?'

'Yeah.'

'So tell me about this fight.'

'He was attacked. He wants to press charges.'

'Hold on, now, Doc. I want to hear what your boy has to say.'

'What he has to say is that he is being bullied in school.'

'I am *not*.'

A radio scanner crackled. The men in the corner had turned off the television. One of them crossed the room and stood beside the uniformed cop.

'This fight, was it with someone you know?'

'No.'

'You sure about that?'

'It was on Hawthorne Row,' Malik said. 'A man he knows had his store burgled and Tariq was there.'

'There *was* a break-in on Hawthorne,' the plain-clothes cop said. 'Phoned in an hour ago. Moran went down.'

Baratelli raised a palm. 'Whoa. Let's all slow down here. Tariq, I want to hear what you got to say. Let's nobody else interrupt.'

They all looked at him. Tariq realised that he was lying about the assault not because he was afraid of Brad and his friend, and not because he was afraid of his father. He was worried about Jamal. He said, 'My friend runs a record store on Hawthorne Row.'

The cops exchanged glances. 'Jamal?' the plain-clothes guy said. 'Jamal Pierce is your friend?'

Tariq nodded. It was the first time he had heard Jamal's last name. 'He texted me to say that someone had broken in. So I cycled down and checked it out. The door was open and stuff and I looked inside. Someone had wrecked the place. But nobody was there.'

'Where was Jamal?'

'I don't know. He wasn't there, that's all I know. So I left and when I went back to my bike some kids were messing with the lock. Trying to steal it. I told them it was mine and we had a fight.'

'How many kids?'

'Two.'

'What did they look like? Describe them.'

'You know. Ordinary looking.'

'White, black, tall, short?'

'White kids. Average height.'

'From your school?'

'No.'

Malik bounced out of his chair. His hair had fallen in front of his eyes and his tie was crooked. 'He is not telling the truth, officer. He has been bullied at school, harassed and bullied to the point where we have had to withdraw him from the high school. Now, obviously the same thugs have done this to him and he is too frightened or weak to admit it. We want to press charges.'

Baratelli carefully placed his clipboard at the corner of his desk and leaned back. 'Dr Mussam, what we need your son to do is give us a detailed description of these other boys and fill out an incident report. And if he does, I can assure you that we will do our best to determine the truth of the situation. Whether he can press charges and so forth.' He turned to Tariq. 'But it's up to him. Is this the truth, son? Have you been kept home from school because of being bullied?'

Tariq pressed his temples with his fingers. He had a fierce headache. 'I got kicked out of school for smoking weed. *That's* the truth.'

The plain-clothes cop gave a little snort and sidled away. The other pushed his chair back from the desk, grimaced and rubbed his forehead with his thumb. 'I suggest the two of you go home and get your story straight. All due respect, Dr Mussam, this isn't a police matter. Not yet anyhow.'

Chapter 22

Sent you mail. Pls read. Rachel.

THE WORDS of the text shimmered in his mind as he showered and dressed and ate breakfast. It had snowed heavily during the night, and the house was unnaturally bright with reflected light. Small birds flashed in the clear sky and every few minutes a clump of snow would fall from the pine trees outside the Greenbriars' house and land with a soft thud.

After an hour he logged on. Seeing her name in his inbox made his heart jump. *Want to see you*, said the subject line.

> Hi Tariq
>
> I heard about your uncle's death and wanted to tell you how sorry I was. I know how close you were to him. He sounded like a great guy, and I wish I'd had the opportunity to meet him.
>
> I started to call you a thousand times and just never went through with it. I suppose you could say I'm a coward, but honestly I wasn't sure what I would say to you. There were questions I wanted to ask you, I do know that, and I guess you would know what those might be. But that didn't really seem fair, under the circumstances.
>
> So first of all – sorry. That day in your house was such a huge disconnect. I guess I wasn't really taking into mind your situation. The crash on the bike, the thing with

school, whatever. I wasn't the most sensitive person on that day and said some things I shouldn't have.

I really would like to see you. I miss you. You must know by now that I have special feelings for you. How many ways do I have to say it? And I need to know if you have them for me. I also need your help about certain decisions and I hope you could use my help too – not that I will tell you what to do. But my sense is that you could use somebody to talk to. And life is so weird without you at school.

So – call me?

Love, Rachel

P.S. Jorgensen hasn't been in school for two weeks and rumour is he's dropped out.

He read the mail three times before shutting down his laptop. He sat before the empty screen for a long time, listening to the scrape of snow shovels from the street below, touching the scabs on his face. The sun sparkled through beads of condensation on his bedroom window. In the kitchen the refrigerator rumbled to life.

Unable to drive home, his father had slept at the hospital. His mother had left early for college to collect her books and papers as end-of-term exams started the next day. It had been such a relief to be alone in the house. The solitude and deep snow had brought a sense of shelter, as if the forces ranged against him had been stilled by nature. He had felt safe. Barricaded. But Rachel's mail was like a brick through a window. Her words reminded him of all that he wanted and couldn't have. And all he didn't want but couldn't escape.

Tariq had not left home since returning from the police station. The atmosphere was anonymous. He and his parents moved through each day as if without a common language, mutely passing each other as they moved from room to room, eating meals alone and at random. Strangely, he privately continued *salat*, laying his prayer mat at the foot of his bed five times each day, washing himself carefully beforehand. The hour or so leading to prayer was often stressful; afterwards he felt protected.

But not this morning. Downstairs he pulled on his boots, took his parka from the hall closet and walked out into the white city. A foot or more of snow layered the streets, capping fence posts, icing electricity lines and bending the branches of the trees along the avenue. He trudged along, breathing in the damp smells and squinting against the reflected sun. The day was clear and windless, with the creaking hush that follows a big snowfall. The cold air made the wounds in his head throb.

Most of the sidewalks remained uncleared, so he walked the border of the gritted street, alongside the curled, crested banks left by the snow ploughs. He tried to recall the time when he and Rachel had been easy with each other. Their private jokes and shared concerns. He wondered how he had allowed this gap between them to grow. Why he couldn't respond to her mail with simple words of his own, telling her that in spite of his efforts, he couldn't stop his heart pounding when she wrote the things she did.

But he couldn't separate his feelings for her from the rest of his life. His entire predicament was of a piece: the bullying, the break-in, life at home and at school. Rahim's death. It was like a jazz tune, each instrument playing its own line but the whole sound making mysterious sense. Rahim had often told him: *Listen to the chords, Rickey. That's where life comes together.* But what if your life came together in despair?

How he missed his uncle. So unlike his father, the imam, the male teachers at the school. Always at peace no matter his burden. Full of energy and wisdom. Tariq regretted not asking him for advice about Rachel. Though he knew what he would have said: *Call her. Ask her out. Enjoy life!*

He walked without purpose, alone with his thoughts. The air glistened. The birds swooped from the eaves. The sky was large and pure. And gradually he saw that he was headed for Jamal's. The only person in as much trouble as he was. The only one who could understand.

The day after the break-in, Tariq had phoned the coffee shop and asked Russell if he had seen him.

'Hide nor hair,' Russell had said. 'And his cell phone's disconnected. Police were poking around the shop yesterday and city maintenance guys came last night and boarded it up.'

'Do you think I should go out to his place?'

'Wouldn't recommend it. You don't go into Jamal's cave without an invite. Bide your time, young fellow. Lick your wounds. He'll come out when he's ready.'

But Tariq couldn't wait. Last night he had dreamed of Jamal leading the high-school band, dramatically waving two arms as they played something brassy and indefinable and Tariq struggled with a saxophone, getting the fingering all wrong and waiting for Jamal to bring the whole piece to a halt and tell him what to do. A conductor. Tariq took that as a sign.

He walked into the town centre, snow crunching beneath his boots. The only vehicles on the roads were city ploughs and four-by-fours. He passed the railway yard and followed the millrace to the west-side bridge. Though the canal was covered in snow, he could hear water flowing. The landscape was entirely black and white, and the dark, wet branches of the bare trees reached skyward like the arms of a preacher.

Two blocks from Jamal's house, Tariq bumped into him coming out of a liquor store. He wore army fatigues, unlaced boots, a sheepskin hat. He carried a bottle wrapped in brown paper by the neck, like a club. Caught off guard, he stepped back, his face creased and truculent. His breath billowed in the bright air, reeking of alcohol.

'I was coming for a visit,' Tariq said.

Jamal moved laterally up the sidewalk, his back to the store wall. He flared his nostrils and lifted his shoulders, like a cornered animal.

'Who told you to do that?'

'To come *see* you?'

Jamal shook his head. 'Don't fuck with me, kid. I know what they're doing. Wait till I'm out of my crib and then send you. Know better than to show their own faces.'

He moved away quickly, the ear-flaps of his hat bobbing in time with his stride.

Tariq puzzled over his words and ran after him. It was as if Jamal hadn't recognised him. 'Nobody sent me,' he shouted. 'Are you OK?'

Jamal ignored him, shuffling through the snow, lifting the bottle every few seconds as if ringing a bell. In his neighbourhood the streets had not yet been ploughed, and the peeling houses and ramshackle yards for once looked picturesque, humped and white and flowing, with criss-cross tracks where people had left home for food or supplies. Or liquor.

Jamal did not turn around until he reached his house. Tariq had caught up with him and stood at the foot of the porch. He pulled back his parka hood. Jamal, who had unlocked the door and was shouldering it open, glanced back. He stopped abruptly and pointed at Tariq's head. 'What's this?' he said.

Tariq had forgotten about his wounds, the shaved patches and the bandages. He touched them lightly with his fingers. 'I had an accident.'

Jamal stared, his mouth scrunched up, his hand on the door handle. He looked up and down the street, snorted and said, 'Come inside. And be quick about it.'

His living room was almost empty. Gone were the stacks of magazines and newspapers, the dusty furniture, the scattered clothes. The hardwood floor had been cleared of everything except the stereo, a few records and a single mattress, neatly made up in the corner. Beside the mattress was an unshaded lamp, a notebook and pen, and, leaning against the wall, a rifle.

Jamal left his boots at the door and brushed snow from his pants legs. He set the wrapped bottle on the floor and hung his army jacket on a hook in the wall. Pale rectangles marked where the jazz posters had been taken down. Dust balls lined the baseboards. Grasping Tariq's shoulder roughly, he examined the bandages and peered into his face. 'Someone gave you a beating.'

'That,' Tariq said, pointing at the gun. 'Is it loaded?'

Jamal let go of his shoulder. 'No point it being unloaded, now, is there?'

'Are you all right, Jamal?'

He licked his top teeth with his tongue, his eyes roving. But his voice was steady as a newsreader's: 'I'm not the one got my head stove in.'

The room smelled of whiskey. The window shades were drawn. The emptiness was disconcerting. Conspiratorial.

'I went down to your store,' Tariq said. 'I saw what happened.'

'Oh yeah?'

'I'm sorry.'

Jamal poked the air with a finger. 'Sorry for what? You think I give a shit about the store? They want to play that game, I say bring it on. You can tell them that.'

'Tell who?'

'You know who. The guys who've been following me. Who sent you here.'

'Nobody sent me.'

Jamal crossed the room and sat cross-legged on his mattress. Back like a ramrod, he grasped the rifle by its barrel, slinging it forward so that it settled on his lap. It was as if he was getting ready to record a video stating terms and conditions. The terrorist in his cave. Tariq stood in the middle of the room; there was nowhere else to sit. Jamal's shaved head stared at the opposite wall, stark as an icon. The shaded windows glowed with the white light of winter.

'Do you think I had something to do with it?' Tariq said.

Jamal smirked. 'I don't put nothing past those guys. They try to get my money any which way they can. But they have no idea who they dealing with.'

'You think the authorities wrecked your store, Jamal? And sent me?'

'If you're not part of the solution, you're part of the problem.'

'Brad and his friend, that was who did it. The guy who you kicked into the pond. They tricked me into going there, they wrecked your place, and then they beat me up.'

He waited for a response, but Jamal continued staring, hands combat-ready. Sweating, Tariq let his parka slide to the floor. 'Don't you have anything to say to that? Aren't you mad at them for what they did? To you? To me?'

Jamal stuck out his lower lip and shook his head again. 'I don't get mad any more. That was my problem. All that shouting and scheming. And then it hits me: let them come to me. If they dare. Let then come and see what a hornets' nest they done stirred up.'

'Let who come, Brad and his friend? They're not going to come here.'

'No? Then you ain't read the same letters *I* have.'

'What letters?'

'Shit. You don't fool me. I let you in for one reason. You my messenger. Go back and tell them I know what's going on. That they done poisoned my food. Listened in on my phone. Talked outside my window at night.'

Tariq weighed up the disconnected phrases, the floating voice, the dead stare. Jamal had been his last hope. Someone who would take him in. Now this. Everything upside down. Then, following the line of Jamal's gaze, he noticed something he hadn't seen before. Taped to the empty wall, about hip-height, was a photograph. Even from across the room he could see that it was an army picture. Three soldiers against a desert landscape. Their war faces on. He stepped closer. Jamal in the middle, two-armed, bare-headed, eyes crinkled against a ferocious sun. His buddies on either side, in sunglasses and camouflage caps, one with a cigarette in his mouth, the other with a hand on Jamal's shoulder. All grimacing with false bravado. Or fear.

Tariq had a sudden vision of Brad and Ronny cowering within aim of Jamal's rifle.

'Jamal,' he said. 'I'm scared.'

'Like to help you, buddy,' Jamal said, his face screwing tighter. 'But the way it's come down, shit, it's every man for himself.'

Chapter 23

Sahar Nassam

(720) 555-4839

TARIQ sat on his bed, flipping the business card with his fingers. He had looked at it often enough to memorise the telephone number. A hollow, falling feeling filled his stomach.

When you're ready to do something about it, Sahar had said, *give me a call*.

He was ready. But questions tumbled through his head: What sort of help was he offering? Was it legal? Was it violent? Sahar worked for a pharmaceutical company. Were there drugs involved? Poisons? What kind of double life did he live?

Since his visit to Jamal, Tariq felt as if sucked into a whirlpool. Circumstances were less and less within his control. He had no allies but Rachel and he was doing everything to keep her at a distance. Meanwhile, the men in his life were deserting him, one by one.

Before leaving for work that morning, his father had called him into the living room. His mother sat on the divan, hands folded in her lap. She was wearing Western clothes. And make-up.

'I have decided to go to Mecca,' he said.

'On *hajj*?'

'Yes. I leave next week and I'll be gone until after the new year.'

His father made this announcement triumphantly, as if he had completed a marathon or climbed a mountain. His face was brighter and clearer than it had been in weeks. His suit was clean.

He had trimmed his nails and got a haircut.

'Isn't this kind of sudden?' Tariq said.

He glanced at his mother. Her face gave no clue to her feelings. Uncovered, her hair was dark and lustrous. Beside her grim, ascetic husband, she looked glamorous.

'As you know,' Malik said, 'I must make *hajj* once in my lifetime ... as you must yourself. As you will someday. But now is the right time for me. Losing Rahim was a great hardship – for all of us, of course, but he was my only brother. There have been difficulties at the hospital. And then all this...' He frowned and spread his arms wide to indicate Tariq's predicament. As if his son's shame had seeped to every corner of the house.

'What about me?' Tariq said.

Malik shrugged. 'You won't tell your parents the truth. You won't tell the police the truth. If you wish to attend the mosque school after al-Hijra you must stop the falsehoods. Allah promises the honest person generous rewards in his first and second lives. Lying brings no reward. So I'm instructing you: while I am away, say your prayers and reconsider your attitude to authority.' He looked at Zaida. 'It is out of my hands.'

He picked up his satchel and left the room, as he would soon be leaving the country. When Tariq turned to his mother she smiled. 'It's something he believes he must do.'

'Obviously.'

'Be patient, Tariq. All will be well.'

He had rarely seen her look so relaxed.

'That's easy for you to say,' he said.

HE called the number on the card. Isn't that what a good Muslim would do? Turn to his own? Sahar sounded unsurprised to hear from him and suggested they meet in an hour at the food court in Cloverleaf Mall.

He was rougher looking than Tariq remembered; instead of pressed white shirt and suit pants or silk *dishdasha*, he wore jeans, a black T-shirt and a leather jacket. His eyes were red-rimmed and his skin dry, as if he hadn't slept well. Not the successful young executive but a pale, restless man adrift in a suburban mall on a weekday.

He fidgeted at the plastic table, sucking a soft drink through a straw and looking Tariq over. 'Were you in an accident?'

'No. It was those guys I told you about.'

'Those kids from your school? They did *this*?'

Tariq nodded.

'So this is why you finally called me.'

'Yeah.'

'Who have you told?'

'My father took me to the police. He wanted me to press charges. But I didn't tell them anything.'

Sahar rattled the ice cubes in his drink. 'You want a Coke?'

'No, thanks.'

Tariq felt exposed. They sat in the general seating area, surrounded by the gaudy signs and repugnant smells of the fast food outlets. Above them rose a towering atrium, criss-crossed by escalators and banded by the concentric tiers of shopping levels. A space as sumptuous and resonant as any Saudi mosque. Across the gallery was the children's play area, where Mrs Hassan, cloak flapping, had screamed obscenities at the young mothers before she chose to walk into Lake Verona with stones in her pockets.

'This was what I was warning you about,' Sahar said. 'This is how it escalates: from intimidation to violence. And who's there to protect you? Nobody. You were smart not to speak to the cops. They hate us.'

'That's why I called.'

'You did the right thing. But if these kids aren't punished for what they did to you, what's to stop them from doing it again? And again.'

'What can you do?'

Sahar picked up his phone, dialled and said in Arabic, 'We are ready.' He set the phone on the table, beside his keys. 'You have to send them a message,' he said quietly. 'Let them know that what they've done has consequences.'

'It's not like they don't deserve it.'

'And the way we do it is safe. They'll know exactly who they're hearing from, but there's no trail. Nothing that points back to you.'

Beneath his eagerness, Tariq was uneasy. In this bland, open space, the air drenched with piped holiday music, the confidences Sahar had whispered outside the mosque prayer hall were less reassuring. He was speaking of something ugly. Something violent.

'Who exactly is going to…who will these bullies be hearing from?' Tariq asked.

Sahar shook his head. 'You don't need to know. Just give us the names, pay the fee and we take it from there.'

'Fee?'

A clean-shaven man in a Bulls warm-up jacket, jeans and a baseball cap appeared beside them. Tariq thought he was looking for spare change, but he sat in the free chair, hands in his pockets.

Sahar nodded at him. 'Our friend needs some help.'

'That's why I'm here,' the man said.

He spoke in English and slumped like an American, keen to blend in. But Tariq heard the desert in his voice.

'Infidels from his school gave him a beating,' Sahar said. 'Because of who he is.'

'Why am I not surprised?'

Tariq could not guess the man's age. His thin lips and cold gaze disturbed him. Eyes deep-socketed, peering aggressively from beneath the bill of the cap. Shoulders tight, knee bouncing.

'Tariq, this is Abdul,' Sahar said. 'He's here to help.'

Abdul smiled, revealing a space between his front teeth. 'I've seen you at Masjid As-Sunnah,' he said. 'Your father is Malik.'

'That's right.'

'A good man. But old school, yeah?'

Old school? Meaning he beat his son and didn't drink? So how was Abdul different?

'Why are we here?' Tariq asked Sahar. 'What are you proposing?'

'Has he made the down payment?' Abdul said.

'We're at the beginning of the process,' Sahar said. 'I was just going to explain the fee.'

'So explain.'

'Abdul has expenses,' Sahar said. 'And he's taking all the risk. So you pay him five hundred up front and five hundred when it's finished.'

'A *thousand dollars?*'

'You can't put a price on peace of mind,' Abdul said, leaning back in his chair.

'And what does he do for that kind of money?'

'He makes certain you never hear from your enemies again. Guaranteed. Or your money back.'

Sahar could have been selling a car.

'I'm in high school. Where am I supposed to get the money?'

'That's not my problem,' Abdul said.

'Wait a minute,' Sahar said. 'Let's not get ahead of ourselves. If you don't have the cash flow, there's a finance deal I can work. I front you the money, and you pay, say, two points a week, plus whatever off the principal.'

'What is this,' Tariq said, '*The Sopranos?*' He zipped up his jacket and pushed his chair away from the table. He was going to borrow a thousand bucks from Sahar? And give it to *this* man? He stood up. 'I have to go.'

'Wait a minute. Sit down.'

'What now?' Abdul said to Sahar in Arabic. 'You told me it was all arranged.'

'We can make this happen,' Sahar said.

Sahar sputtered on about sticking together, battling discrimination, making the bullies pay. Abdul sat, hands in his pockets, seething.

Feeling watched, Tariq lifted his gaze and saw, a level up, Rachel leaning on the railing and peering down at him. She beckoned and pointed at the escalator. Suddenly, he saw himself through her eyes: childish, confused, alienated. Abdul and Sahar bickered in Arabic. Abdul had raised his voice, and a mall security guard was looking at them.

Tariq edged away. Abdul was thrusting a finger in Sahar's chest. Tariq hopped on the escalator. He felt as if he were being lifted into heaven. Rachel passed him going down. Like kids on a merry-go-round, they giggled and pointed at each other. 'Wait for me up there,' she shouted.

At the top he watched her float back to him, face upturned like a flower in the sun. They hugged unabashedly. It was as if all the tension between them had never been.

'What were you *doing* down there?' she said.

'You don't want to know.'

Abdul and Sahar were walking towards the exit while the security guard spoke into a walkie-talkie.

'Friends of yours?' she asked.

'These days, you're my only friend.'

'You know who that is?'

'Who?'

'The guy in the basketball jacket.'

'Abdul.'

'His name's not Abdul. It's Keith. He's a drug dealer.'

'How do you know that?'

'Everyone knows it. He's, like, Annalise's main supplier.'

'Great. It all connects.'

'What do you mean?'

'It doesn't matter.'

Rachel was staring at him. She stood there bright-eyed, lips slightly parted, holding an Aéropostale bag and smoothing her denim skirt against her thigh with her free hand.

'And what's all this?' she said, delicately touching the wounds on his face and pointing at the bandages.

'I've got a lot to tell you,' he said. 'I'm sorry I never replied to your email.'

'That's OK. Why don't we get some coffee?'

'Not here.'

She turned her head in both directions, distracted, as if just discovering where she was. 'My car's outside,' she said.

Chapter 24

THEY DROVE to her house. Not in the family Land Cruiser but an old Volkswagen. The snow had melted, leaving streaks of grit along the edges of the roads and patches of dirty ice in the shade of buildings. But it was cold, and the car's heating didn't work. So cold he was shaking.

But she appeared comfortable, driving casually, one wrist draped over the steering wheel, her plastic bracelets clicking as she shifted gears. She wore a duffel coat that didn't quite go with the funky skirt and black tights, fashionably laddered along her calf. Her perfume was lighter than when he had met her last, the day of his bicycle accident, her hair a little wild.

Also, she wore her glasses.

'You're not wearing your new contacts.'

'No,' she said. 'They dried out my eyes.'

'I like your glasses.'

She glanced at him sidelong and smiled. 'All the better to see you with, my dear.'

Tariq had never been to her house. Her parents were both lawyers, and the family lived in Crestwood, where each home was lavish but eco-friendly, with solar panels and triple-glaze windows and plenty of wooded space between properties. The good life guilt-free, Rachel liked to say. The house was open-plan, full of books, contemporary paintings, a Steinway. Lots of light. A menorah on the dining table. A cat meowed, rubbing against his legs.

'Osiris,' she said, 'go away.'

Unable to keep still, he wandered the space, rubbing surfaces, touching objects, comparing it all, against his will, with the ornate pink living room at home. Which she had called a bordello.

'Where is everybody?' he said.

'My parents left this morning for Milwaukee. My dad has a conference and they decided to stay overnight.'

The tension sharpened. Already he was on a knife edge. On the ride over they had avoided the raw subjects that lay between them. His wounds, inside and out. Their last meeting. Her texts and mails. The future. The evasion had continued after they arrived. But now, as he looked through a huge pane of glass at the broad expanse of back lawn and high screen of junipers, she touched his shoulder. He didn't look at her.

'You're very accident-prone these days,' she said.

'That's one way of looking at it.'

'Are you going to tell me what happened?'

'Well, it wasn't a bike crash.'

'Was it them?'

He turned around. Her eyes and lips were glistening. 'Yes,' he said.

Haltingly, she reached across and laid a hand on his chest. Her eyes flared when she felt the thumping of his heart. His face was hot, and he stepped back, avoiding her gaze.

'I'll make tea,' she said.

She let the cat out the back and went into the kitchen. He followed, stirred by her touch, bursting with all he wanted to say. While she busied herself with the kettle and cups and a tin of Earl Grey, he sat at the dining table and told her the story of the attack: the phony text message, the mess, the fear. Being rescued by Russell. The police station.

She poured the tea and sat across from him.

'How am I supposed to think about school with stuff like this going on?' he said.

'I don't know.'

'And you know what the weirdest thing is? I kept doing my homework. Wessell would send it and I would do it and send it back. Brad and his friend are mashing me on the head with a two-by-four and for some reason I think it's wrong if I don't do my algebra.'

'Do you still want to go to the mosque school?'

The answer became clear to him only as he said the words.

'No,' he said, 'I don't. But how can I go back to Monroe High? Those guys might kill me. If Jamal doesn't kill them first.'

'What are you talking about?'

He told her about Jamal's locker full of weapons, his drinking and paranoia. The episode at the quarry. 'This whole thing is like I wandered into a movie. But it's real life. Poor Jamal. Who's going to help him? He's holed up in his house, desperate and sick, and there I am in Cloverleaf Mall, negotiating with some guy named Abdul about doing who knows what to a couple of high-school kids.'

'Well, they did beat you up.' She reached across the table and grasped his hand. 'Do you think you *should* go to the police? If these things you're saying are true.'

'Of *course* they're true. Do you think I'm imagining it?'

'That's not what I meant,' she said.

He was too wound up to stay seated. He paced the floor. 'Maybe Jamal has it right: batten down the hatches, don't talk to anybody, keep the blinds down and the guns loaded.'

She stood up and caught him as he went past, locking her arms around him and pinning his own against his ribs. 'C'mon, now,' she said, 'this is crazy. You're getting melodramatic.'

He felt her breasts push against his chest. The smell of her hair made him dizzy. 'And I didn't answer your mail,' he whispered in her ear. 'Or your texts. You were the only one trying to help me and I acted like you weren't there.'

'Hey. Quiet. It doesn't matter.'

She loosened her grip and leaned back, smiling, arms still around his shoulders. And he kissed her.

It was an awkward kiss. His nose bumped her glasses and his teeth knocked against hers. But her breathing was heavy and her perfume was rich and arousing and all the stress of the last four months seemed to collect in his chest and flow into his limbs and whet his desire.

She stepped back. The space between them was dense with the drama of what they had done. She touched her lips.

'What am I going to do?' he said.

'You mean right *now*?'

He laughed nervously. 'I guess I meant more generally.'

She took off her glasses and cleaned the smudged lens with her shirttail. Pursed her lips and swallowed. Finally she said, 'Are you hungry? Why don't I make us something to eat.'

'Sure.'

And so they found, for the moment, the distance needed to assess where they had so suddenly landed. But the smallest actions were magnified. He watched as she made sandwiches, cutting tomatoes, spreading mayonnaise onto the bread, talking while she worked in rhythms not quite suited to her words, quick and clipped, like a musician rushing a tune. Don't worry, she told him, *she* was there. He could go back to school, he could start afresh. She asked him to set the table, and as he fetched plates and napkins they avoided brushing against each other with comic exaggeration, frightened by the passions they had loosed.

They ate. He talked about Rahim's death, his father's planned pilgrimage and his mother's remove. His music. The words poured from him as if from a swollen river, details rushing past as she listened and murmured and shook her head.

Afterwards they cleaned up and went into the beamed, high-ceilinged living room, where the echo of their kiss expanded in the larger space and made them even more awkward. She sat at the piano and played some slight classical tune. Not well, but competently. It was like a parody of a scene from Jane Austen. At the keyboard she looked uncertain but elegant, her elbows tucked in at her sides, her ballet shoes working the pedals, her fingers stiff and uncertain.

When she finished she stared at the keyboard. 'If you had your clarinet,' she said, 'we could have played a duet. Did you get it fixed?'

'Yes.'

'Are you practising?'

'A little.'

'Oh,' she said, jumping up from the stool, 'I *knew* there was something I wanted to show you. Come with me.'

She grabbed his hand and pulled him along. They went upstairs to her room. The move did not seem calculated; she was full of spontaneous energy and excitement.

He had never been in a girl's bedroom. The bed was unmade. Clothing was strewn on the floor and bottles of make-up and brushes and soiled cotton pads littered the dresser-top. On the wall was a poster of a polar bear and her cub.

She seemed not to notice the mess. 'Sit,' she said, directing him to the edge of the bed while she rummaged through CDs piled on her desk beside a portable player.

She stopped. 'I can't seem to find it.'

'What?'

'It's a surprise.'

She opened a drawer. 'Well, this isn't what I was looking for, but...'

She lifted a plastic baggie full of weed.

'I didn't know you were into that,' he said.

'No more than you are. You know, you haven't told me about your episode in the bathroom at school. You nearly gave Annalise a heart attack. She thought you were going to narc on her.'

'I'm sure she got over it.'

She shook the bag. 'Shall we?'

'I don't think so.'

'You can't tell me you haven't tried it before.'

'I didn't inhale.'

Her mouth dropped open. 'What?'

'It was the only way I could get out of going to school.'

'Well, you're going to have to find out what you missed.'

She took a notebook from the desk, opened it and sat beside him on the bed, her hip pressed against his. She took papers from the drawer and rolled a joint in the fold of the notebook, tilting the excess buds and leaves back into the baggie when she was finished. It wasn't the first time she had done it. She smelled the joint, moistened it with her lips, and lit it. After a long toke she handed it to him.

When he hesitated, she exhaled smoke and said, 'Sumerian monks were doing this five thousand years ago.'

'Is that a fact?'

'Look at it as a part of your heritage you've neglected.'

He had trouble keeping the smoke down and coughed and sputtered a few times. But the effect was immediate. His body tingled and his mouth went dry. Time slowed. Colours intensified, and the whole room shimmered. The polar bear appeared to be moving, and the push of Rachel's hip against his was an event all its own, isolated, intense and in the shape of his desire.

They finished the joint and sat for an immeasurable stretch of time, floating, staring ahead, looking at each other on occasion and giggling for no reason.

She pointed at the floor. '*There* it is.'

'What?'

She bent down and picked up a CD case. Took the disc from its case, set it in the player, and turned it on.

The music exploded. Amazingly, it was *choubi*. He knew the tune at once: 'Oh Mother, the Handsome Man Tortures Me'. Frenzied, clenched, powerful. Reeds and strings whining the melody and a hand drum adding gunfire rhythms. Vocals from deep in the singer's throat, shouting and tearing through the lament. It was Baghdad back-alley. Iraqi punk. Stunning at the most sober of moments, but under the influence of the weed it was like a burst of fireworks.

Rachel danced, bending and stretching and shaking as if the music came from within her. Her glasses had fallen off and her face was lax with ecstasy. Her hands floated like butterflies and her body undulated like a snake. The music and her movement made him want to leap and shout, but he sat still, letting the waves of pleasure flow through him.

The next tune was 'Mother, Here's Beauty', sinuous and dry, full of flirtatiousness. Swaying slightly, Rachel looked down at him, breathing heavily after the dance. She picked up her glasses and set them on the dresser. Then she leaned over him and pushed his chest so that he fell back on the bed. In time with the slow rhythms of the song, she unbuckled his belt and unbuttoned his pants and gently slid them down his hips. She moved above him, on all fours. The ends of her hair grazed his face. The music flowed around them. She kissed him, deeply, and he felt as if swirling in space, removed from everything except the music and her taste and touch, and he pulled her to him and wrapped her in his arms.

Chapter 25

THE SCHOOL BELL was ringing. It wouldn't stop. He rushed through the halls, legs heavy, bumping into other students, who were all walking rigidly in the opposite direction, as if in a zombie movie. He couldn't find his classroom. He couldn't even remember the subject of the class. Beneath his confusion was a sense of dread – Jorgensen was looking for him and might appear at any moment. And still the bell rang, like a spike between his eyes.

He woke. The ringing came from his phone, beside him on the floor. Without knowing where he was, he answered.

'Tariq, where are you?'

His mother. He sat up in the bed. He was naked. Rachel lay beside him, asleep, a breast exposed. He pulled the sheet over her shoulder.

'At a friend's,' he said, his voice hoarse.

'What friend?'

He cleared his throat. 'Nobody you know.'

There was scuffling at the other end of the phone. Voices speaking Arabic. Rachel stirred. She lifted her head and smiled. 'You sleep?' she said.

'Shh.'

'Tariq, this is your father speaking. Come home at once.'

His tone was restrained, as if others could hear him.

'Why?' Tariq said. 'What's going on?'

'The police are here. At the house. They need to speak to you.'

'About what?'

'They won't say. You must come home.'

Tariq hung up, still under the spell of the dream and the warm buzz of the dope. His parents' voices receded into nothingness, like a computer screen gone blank. The room, the bed, the sounds, Rachel's body stretched out beside him – the scene was kaleidoscopic, made up of fragments that refused to come together.

Under the sheet Rachel's hand rested on his thigh. She was still smiling, sleepy-eyed. He stroked her brow, lifting strands of hair from her eyes.

'Where am I?' he said.

She giggled. 'Strong stuff, huh? Maybe too strong for your first time.'

First time. Beneath the unreal shimmer of the high was a warmth in his chest that he knew would stay with him for a long time. It was like the tenderness of heart the imams defined when they spoke of those entitled to paradise.

He checked the time. Six o'clock. They had been asleep for an hour.

'The cops are at my house,' he said.

'Cops? What's wrong?'

'I don't know. I have to go.'

'Hey.' Holding the sheet to her neck, she used her other arm to pull him towards her and slowly kissed him. 'I'm really glad you came over,' she whispered.

'Me too.'

'Do you want a shower?'

'I better go.'

'I'll give you a ride.'

They dressed without looking at each other. Downstairs, Osiris scratched at the glass. Rachel opened the sliding door and the cat streaked inside, followed by a stream of cold air.

In the car they sat shivering. She did not start the engine.

'Are you sure you should be driving?'

'Tariq, I'm not sure of anything.'

SHE dropped him off a block away.

'What will you tell them?'

'The police? I don't know. Come clean, I guess.'

They kissed. He was suddenly nervous.

'Can I call you after this?' he said. 'Maybe see you later?'

'Of course.'

At his house, two policemen sat on the edge of the divan, holding glasses of tea. The room was warm, but they had not removed their leather jackets and their hats rested on the pillow between them. Tariq's father faced them, sitting in the wing chair. One of the cops was the older man who had interviewed Tariq at the station: Officer Baratelli. He stood up when Tariq entered, relieved that the small talk was over, that business could begin.

'You remember me, young fella?' he said, extending a hand.

Tariq shook it, worried that he reeked of marijuana. 'Yes, sir.'

'Your dad here has been telling us about his trip.'

'Trip?'

'To Mecca.'

'Oh, yeah. Sure.'

Hulking and self-conscious in the ornate room, Officer Baratelli stood awkwardly in his stocking feet, swaying slightly on the polished floor. His jacket and holster creaked and his gun sat on his hip like a bird on a fence. Malik sat with his hands folded across his stomach, eyes flitting from one cop to the other. Baratelli's partner was a young blond guy with thin lips and ruddy cheeks.

MAHONEY on his name tag. Sounds came from the kitchen. His mother clearing up.

'Officer, please,' his father said. 'Now that my son is here, what is this about?'

Baratelli grimaced. His face, worn and seamed as an old tree trunk, was framed by aviator glasses with thick lenses.

He cleared his throat. 'Right. Let's sit down, please.'

Trying to concentrate, Tariq pulled a wooden chair from the corner. He could still smell Rachel's perfume. The young cop removed a notebook and pen from his jacket pocket.

'Tariq,' Baratelli said, 'you told me last week that you're a friend of Jamal Pierce.'

'I guess.'

'Have you seen him recently?'

'Does this have anything to do with the break-in?'

'When was the last time you saw Jamal, Tariq?'

'Who is this Jamal?' Malik said, his voice straining. 'Is he a Muslim?'

'About a week ago.'

'Where?'

'At his house.'

'How was he?'

'Not the best.'

'Are you on good terms with him?'

'I *was*. Before.'

'Before what?'

'He's been acting strange lately.'

The young cop made a note.

'How about Brad Jorgensen?' Baratelli said.

'What about him?'

'Do you know him?'

'He's in my school.'

'And you were present when Jamal Pierce and this Jorgensen kid had an altercation? At the quarry?'

'Who told you that?'

'Were you, Tariq?'

'Yes. But there's more to it than that.'

'I'm sure there is.'

Baratelli hung his head for a moment then spread his hands. 'Look, it's going to be on television soon if it's not already. Every station in town is down there. Your friend Pierce is holding this kid Jorgensen hostage. In Pierce's house.'

'*What?*'

Malik sat bolt upright. Tariq's mother, who had moved into the kitchen doorway, gasped. She stood with one hand on the lintel and the other clutching a dish-towel.

'These are people you *know?*' his father said to Tariq.

'It's a bad situation,' Baratelli said. 'Pierce is an angry man. Has been for a while. There's an ongoing dispute with the city about taxes – maybe he mentioned it to you – and yesterday the sheriff went out to serve a lien. No sign of anyone there, place locked up tight as a drum. Then this afternoon, Allen gets a call.' He nodded at his partner. 'Friend of Jorgensen named Ronny Fish, all hysterical.'

Mahoney picked up the narrative. 'Fish claimed that Pierce abducted Jorgensen at gunpoint. In the parking lot at Target. Forced him to drive away. So we go out to Pierce's house. Not me, but an earlier shift. The car was there, the windshield smashed. It was verified that the perpetrator and hostage were in the perp's house. There were words exchanged. I understand that a weapon was produced.'

'Cut a long story short,' Baratelli said, 'it's going on two hours now and a SWAT team's on its way from Milwaukee. It's not good.'

Malik said, 'Officer, this is all news to my wife and me. We had no idea our son was associating with criminals.'

'Jamal is not a criminal,' said Tariq.

'Hold on, everybody,' Baratelli said.

'This has nothing to do with my son. Do you understand? We are a peaceful family. We mind our own business.'

'Listen to me. Pierce is a veteran. I'm a vet myself. I know post-traumatic stress when I see it. And we've got a psychiatrist on the scene. But if we're not careful here the whole thing could blow up in our face. These SWAT guys aren't paid for their sensitivity.'

'Officer,' Malik said, 'you must be the one who listens. This has nothing to do with us.'

'Oh, but it does, Mr Mussam. He wants to talk to Tariq. Jamal does.'

'Tariq?'

'Says he'll only negotiate through him.'

'*Negotiate?*' Zaida said.

Baratelli shook his head. 'It's not my word, it's Pierce's. But it *is* a hostage situation. If you could talk to him, Tariq, it might help.'

Tariq looked at his father. Malik was calm for once, certain that there could be only one outcome. 'My son is not getting himself involved in any kidnapping incident. Any violent activity.'

Baratelli raised both hands. 'Mr Mussam, don't get me wrong. No-one's suggesting Tariq or anybody else get into the middle of anything here. But we have a phone link set up. A line of communication. If your boy can come to the scene with us and take a call, just a phone call, well, it could defuse a dangerous situation.'

Malik dismissed the explanation with a wave of his hand. And that wave reminded Tariq of the movement his father would make just before he hit him.

'I can call him,' Tariq said.

The words came easily to him. They sounded right.

'No, you can't,' Malik said flatly. 'You're not going anywhere. Zaida, come in here. Officers, you will have to go. I must ask you to leave.'

'I don't need your permission. Isn't that right, officer?'

'And *you* end up as a hostage?' Malik said, his voice straining. 'Do you think I moved you and your mother from Baghdad so that you could get involved with men with guns? *Stress* disorder? Do you think we don't know about stress, officer? About guns and hostages? My son is not leaving this house. Do you understand?'

Baratelli eyed Malik but spoke to Tariq. 'Actually, you *do* need permission. If you're under eighteen.'

Malik sniffed and crossed his arms. He had grown pale.

'I'll give him permission,' Tariq's mother said from the doorway.

The men looked her way. Malik said, 'Don't be foolish, Zaida. He can't go.'

She stepped into the room. 'This man is in danger. This boy also. Malik, what would Rahim have done? If Tariq can help, then he should go.'

Malik shook his head, unable to speak.

Baratelli stood up. 'That OK with you, Tariq?'

Tariq nodded. Malik stared at each of them in turn and walked wordlessly out of the room.

Chapter 26

FROM A DISTANCE, Jamal's neighbourhood had the glow of a funfair: blue strobes flashing, yellow police tape festooning the lamp-posts, curious neighbours gawking from behind metal barriers. The street had been cordoned off at either end, and fifty yards from the barriers the facade of Jamal's house blazed in the industrial glare of siege lights. City cops had secured the perimeter. Satellite stalks extended, three TV news vans camped behind the crowds, surrounded by a tangle of wires and stands of interview lights and alert reporters with stiff hair. Away from the action, parked under the bare trees, was an ambulance.

Baratelli led Tariq and his mother past the cordon as the crowd murmured and the television cameras swivelled in their direction. Zaida wore Western clothes but also her blue hijab, creating a spark of mystery. As if entering a movie set, they walked to an armoured police van parked crosswise in the street, about twenty yards from Jamal's front door. Beyond the van, behind tree trunks and fence posts opposite the house, crouched three soldiers in body armour and black helmets. Each carried a black assault rifle. The SWAT team had arrived.

When he saw the guns, Tariq's confidence shrivelled. Suddenly the scene was tight and frightening. Plain-clothes officials huddled at the open rear door of the van, including the chief of police, a representative from the mayor's office, a grey-haired negotiating expert and a psychiatrist.

'He's called twice,' the grey-haired man said before they were even introduced. He wore a headset and monitored a stack of electronic gear inside the van. 'We told him the kid was on the way. He doesn't sound too together.'

Tariq recognised the psychiatrist. Her name was Linda Reed and last year she had given a talk on substance abuse at the high school. She looked out of place among the men: younger, like a student herself, with short spiky hair and a nose stud.

The chief's name was Gretch. At first, he scarcely acknowledged Tariq. Above a yellowing moustache, his small eyes were both focused and distant. He held a paper cup of coffee, steaming in the cold, and puffed relentlessly on a cigarette.

'The Milwaukee unit didn't waste any time,' he said quietly to Baratelli.

'How many?'

'Seven.' He pointed at the soldiers. 'These three here, two around the back and one each in the neighbouring houses.'

'Have you cleared the street?'

'Absolutely.'

'Who's in charge?'

The chief nodded at the soldier closest to the van, squatting behind a wooden gate. 'Name's Ahern. He's the incident commander. For now he reports to me, but if we don't make some progress here soon, who knows? The governor has been informed. He's not happy.' He turned to Tariq's mother and his voice switched tone with effortless professionalism. 'Mrs Mussam, we very much appreciate you making your son available for this call. Right now, he's our best shot. We're getting nowhere with Pierce.'

'It is Tariq's decision.'

'Well, son, we're glad you're on board.'

But Tariq was not glad. These men scared him. Their authority was mechanical and unbending. They worried about how they were perceived. And they would leave nothing to fate. What chance did Jamal have against them? He was a loner. With one arm, enough weaponry to make him a target, and a fading grip on what was good for him.

In a flat voice, Chief Gretch told him that when the call came through he was to engage naturally with Jamal and simply ask what he wanted. Make no commitments. Tell him that everyone out here just wanted to help, but they needed to know what it was he needed. He was not to use the words 'hostage' or 'demands'. This wasn't television. And the team would be listening in. There was nothing to worry about.

Linda spoke in a soft voice. 'We've been in touch with the VA. And we're waiting for his records. He has a history of post-traumatic stress but has missed his scheduled reviews at the hospital. He's very unstable right now.'

'Not a good recipe,' the negotiator said, without turning around.

'He lost his arm in an explosion,' Tariq said. 'In Iraq. And two of his friends were killed.'

'He told you that?' the chief said.

'Isn't it true?'

Linda lifted her hands. 'I don't have the file yet.'

'Well, we don't have all night,' the chief said.

The men remained tight-lipped and hunched, waiting for the phone to ring.

'You're from Baghdad,' Linda said to Zaida, 'isn't that right?'

Tariq's mother nodded. Tariq sensed judgement and distance from the men. In spite of everything, he wished his father was here. Or Rahim. He felt unprotected. As if he were the one under siege.

He took a step back. The glare of the siege lights rimmed the roof of the police van like the bright band on the horizon right after sundown. The light blotted out the sky and outlined the bare trees with twisted clarity. From the van came the click of technology and the low voices of the men. To Tariq the situation was both terrifying and unreal. Like so many American scenes – pep rallies at the high school, holiday parades, sales presentations in department stores – it felt scripted. As if it *were* television. And yet there it all was: guns and armour, satellite technology, rules of engagement. The governor had been informed.

'If Jamal has post-traumatic stress,' Tariq said, interrupting his mother, 'is it really a good idea to have soldiers around his house?'

Before anyone could reply, the negotiator lifted his hand. 'It's ringing,' he said. Tariq couldn't hear anything, but red and green lights were flashing on the monitor.

The negotiator spoke into the headset. 'Yes ... that's right, Jamal, he's here ... no, no, he wants to talk to you ... wait, please.'

The chief, who had also donned a headset, handed Tariq a cell phone.

'Hello?' Tariq said.

For a moment there was only the surfing sound of telephone static and the thud of Tariq's heartbeat in his ears. Then Jamal said, 'Liquorice stick man.'

'Hi, Jamal.'

'I interrupt your practising?'

'No.'

'Just another day in the life, huh? I don't expect you woke up this morning thinking *this* shit was going to fall your way.'

Tariq pictured waking beside Rachel, the lashes of her closed eyes long and dark, the curve of her shoulders pink and translucent, like the skin of an apricot.

'No ... I guess.'

'OK. Right. I know the drill, and I know those motherfuckers

225

are right there beside you, listening in. Be telling you what to tell me, everything is cool, all shit like that. But save your breath.'

'What can I do, Jamal? I just want to help.'

There was a pause while Jamal weighed the question. The monitor hummed and whirred and the lights blinked.

'Come on in. We need to talk.'

The negotiator had a diagram board and with a black marker scrawled ASK HIM TALK ABOUT WHAT?

'Yeah,' Tariq said to Jamal. 'I can do that.'

'Just you, liquorice. No funny business with the man. I'm locked and loaded in here.'

The line went dead.

'You can do what?' his mother said at once.

She had grasped his arm so tightly it hurt. Within the folds of the hijab her face was dark and pinched.

'He wants me to go in.'

The chief had the headset off, another cigarette lit. 'Let's slow down here. Tariq, you didn't ask him what he wanted. This is step one. Let's wait for him to call back.'

'What he wants is for me to go into the house.'

'Not a good idea.'

'If I don't go in now, he won't trust me. Like he doesn't trust you.'

'*Habibi*,' his mother whispered. She drew him aside. 'What are you doing?'

'Ommi, he's my friend.'

'He's armed.'

'Everybody's armed. He has someone in there and he wants to talk to me. Let me go in. It will be all right. It's what Ammu Rahim would have done.'

She sighed and grasped his hand. Her fingers trembled. 'Your father loves you.'

'I know.'

'He is worried about you.'

'Let me go in, Ommi.'

She looked at the house, the SWAT team, the van. 'Mr Baratelli,' she said at last. 'My son wants to see his friend.'

JAMAL unlatched the door and stepped back into the gloom of his living room. He told Tariq to lock up behind him and slide the wooden chest in front of the door. The room was cold. When Tariq's eyes had grown used to the murk, he saw Brad sitting on the floor against the right-hand wall, near the stereo. His wrist was attached to a radiator pipe with a plastic tie and he was staring at his bare feet.

Then the guns. Surrounding Jamal's mattress were the weapons from the locked cupboard – blunt, gleaming, smelling of oil and solvent. Handguns, rifles, a shotgun, boxes of ammunition. Jamal resettled himself amid the hardware, looking like an African warlord. He wore battle fatigues and black boots. A red scarf around his neck. He picked up a rifle and rested it on his thigh, pointed at Brad.

'What did they tell you out there, Tariq? Don't bullshit me, now.'

'To be careful.'

They had also told him to note the layout of the house and the position of Jamal and Brad, to ask questions instead of making statements, to agree rather than disagree. And they offered him a bulletproof vest. He had declined.

Jamal laughed mirthlessly. 'Why's that? *You* ain't the one in danger.'

He spat on the floor. The room was dirtier than the last time Tariq had been here. Scuff marks on the walls. Water stains on the floor. A hole in the ceiling. There was a smell of garbage and liquor. And urine.

'Hey,' Jamal shouted at Brad, 'where's your manners? We got a guest.'

Brad shifted his position but did not speak or lift his head. One of the smells came from him – the crotch of his pants had darkened where he'd pissed himself. Without appearing to stare, Tariq tried to see if he was hurt, but there was no sign of blood or bruising.

'Big man Brad done lost his voice. Where's your swagger now, motherfucker?'

Tariq moved closer to Jamal. His eyes were bloodshot, his cheeks unshaven. His voice was hoarse and the flesh of his face loose. His lower lip, moist and red, hung down when he wasn't speaking. A cell phone lay on the soiled mattress. On the floor was a half-empty bottle of Jim Beam, cap off.

He spoke softly. 'Jamal, I'm worried.'

'That a fact?'

'These men outside, they don't mess around.'

Jamal snorted. Took a swig of the whiskey. 'What do you call this shit that's been my life? I try to do the right thing, the moral thing, and I get harassed by the government, I get my business destroyed, I get my home surrounded. If that ain't a mess-around, what is?'

'I don't want to see you get hurt.'

His face went stony and he waved Tariq aside. 'Move out of the way, you blocking my view of the prisoner.'

He spat again. 'Hey, motherfucker. How much you think those records you smashed was worth? How much you think you owe me?'

Brad breathed in spasms. He wore only a torn T-shirt and shivered in the chill. He kept his head lowered, and a fringe of hair hid his eyes.

'Shoulda heard this shitbag when I met him in the parking lot. What he wasn't going to do to my black ass. Ain't talking now, is he? Ain't calling me *psycho* and ain't calling you *freak*.'

These outbursts drained more energy from Jamal's wilted frame. When he turned his attention from Brad, his features sagged and softened and his eyes were like those of a sick dog. Tariq got down on one knee so that his face was level with Jamal's. 'Have you had anything to eat today? You want me to make you something?'

'Who do you think you are – the pizza man in *Dog Day Afternoon*? Shit, I got Mr Beam here, all the calories *I* need.'

Jamal strove for jocularity, but his voice was tight as a guy-line. The muscles in his face seethed.

'They have a SWAT team out there,' Tariq said under his breath. 'Surrounding the house.'

Now *he* was sounding like television.

'Do tell,' Jamal said.

'You can't just sit here and wait for something to happen.'

'I don't intend to.'

Jamal shifted the rifle on his lap and wiped his nose with his sleeve. Backlit by the powerful lights outside, the shaded windows glowed like ghost images after a camera flash.

'You telling me it's decision time,' Jamal said.

'I'm saying think about what's happening here. What *could* happen.'

'OK. So let's take it to the next level. You the man, Tariq. You tell me what to do.'

'Really?'

'Really. Starting with Brad over there. You say the word and it's done.'

From Brad came a barely audible whimper. The empty room

was like a stage, the three of them a tense triangle of actors with no lines left to recite. Climax beckoned.

'You promise?' Tariq whispered.

'I promise. Now's the time. All the misery he done put you through. Put me through. The hurt he caused.'

For the first time, Brad looked up. Tariq was surprised. He expected to see defeat in his eyes, but his gaze was bright with unrepentant savagery. Still the bully. Still out to intimidate. In spite of the protection of shackles and guns, Tariq felt a reflex of fear in his stomach.

'Anything I want?' Tariq said.

'Your wish is my command. You want to kick his ass, kick it. You want me to shoot the motherfucker in the foot, just tell me. Whatever.'

Jamal's gold tooth caught the muted light. His head slumped between his shoulders and his scraggly beard was dirty and uneven. He looked like an old vulture. Tariq remembered the first time they had met, when Jamal's energy and colourful clothes and ringing voice had rescued him from despair. Now his eyes were watery and dull and his bald head was like a skull. All light and music were gone. In their place a tuneless chant of rage.

'Let him go,' Tariq said.

Jamal shook his head. Flared his nostrils. 'Be serious.'

'I am serious.'

Jamal held up a heavy plastic club. 'Teach him a lesson.'

'I said let him go, Jamal.'

His shoulders jigged. He bared his teeth. He fumed. 'Shit. After what he did to you? To me?'

'Enough is enough.'

'Enough? Nothing ain't enough, man. Minimum, I say give him a hiding.'

'Why, so they can bring even more charges against you?'

In his agitation, Jamal kicked the bottle over. He cursed as he righted it. Spat again in Brad's direction. 'Everything what's gone down today,' he said, 'they got plenty to charge me with. Fucking up this cracker ain't going to make no difference.'

'You promised, Jamal.'

Jamal went still, closing his eyes and breathing with controlled ferocity. Brad shifted. Sniffled.

Unbidden, a line from the Hadith rose to Tariq's lips: *The prophet was ever ready to forgive his enemies.*

Jamal grimaced and looked away. He slid his hand beneath the mattress and withdrew a pair of wire-cutters. He handed them to Tariq, who crossed the room, trembling, and snipped Brad free. Brad rubbed his wrist and stared at Jamal, afraid to move.

'Go ahead,' Tariq said. 'Get out of here.'

'I don't trust him,' Brad said.

'So you're going to wait for him to shoot you? Go out there and tell them not to do anything until we call. I'm the hostage now.'

Bare-footed, Brad hobbled out. Shouts and commotion rang and faded as Tariq locked the door and slid the chest back into place. Moving the guns aside, he sat beside Jamal on the mattress.

They did not speak for several minutes. Tariq was reminded of the last time he saw Rahim. Instead of hospital light and oxygen tanks it was mottled walls and ordnance, but the same smell of death was in the air.

'You got it all worked out, don't you, liquorice stick man?'

'No I don't.'

Jamal was silently crying, his lone hand cradling his chin. He was as crushed and vulnerable as he had been returning from his encounter with Charmaine. Worse.

'Can I make a suggestion?' Tariq said.

'No, you can't. My turn.' Jamal wiped his eyes and swivelled on the mattress so that he faced Tariq squarely. 'You're my suicide note,' he said.

'What does that mean?'

'It means you go back out there and tell them my story. You're the only one knows it. You tell it to the papers so the world knows. You make sure they know the truth about Jamal Pierce.'

'And what do you do?'

'What I have to.'

Tariq could hardly look at him. The curve of his bald head, the broad nose, the looseness of his mouth and the way the tremble of his moist lower lip was echoed by the wisp of beard – it was as if, for the first time, Tariq could see Jamal's true self. Rahim wrapped suffering around his shoulders like a cloak, but Jamal was a man dying of thirst in the desert. Looking skyward for God but finding only a cruel sun. And Tariq knew that the cast of his own fear was closer to Jamal's than Rahim's. His uncle had found strength in hatred. But Jamal's predicament had no enemy but the way of the world. No solution but self-harm.

'I can't do that,' Tariq said.

'I ain't asking. I'm telling.'

'And what if I don't?'

Jamal put his hand on the stock of the rifle. 'You really want to be here for this?'

His face had hardened, determination overcoming desperation. Tariq stood and moved to the middle of the room. Jamal picked up the cell phone and skipped it across the floor. 'Call them,' he said. 'Tell them you coming out. Tell them you got the situation in hand. Because you do, liquorice. You the man now.'

In the white heat of the moment, Tariq heard a chord. It echoed in his head. Then Rahim's voice. *Play through the sound. Like the wind through the trees.*

He went to the pile of records beside the stereo and sorted through them rapidly, scattering the covers.

'What the fuck you doing?' Jamal said.

They were all here: Ellington, Mingus, Miles, Rahsaan. The sweet thunder that had shaken the walls of Jamal's shop and gripped Tariq's soul.

'Don't mess with me, Tariq. I ain't in no mood.'

Tariq found *A Love Supreme* and slid the vinyl from its sleeve. He put it on the turntable and turned up the volume.

The saxophone was like the call of a muezzin. Like the voice of Allah. In the hothouse funk of the low-ceilinged room, crammed with the tools of violence and the stink of failure, its emotion was almost too much to bear. The clenched, twisting notes. The transcendent declamations. It could not be denied.

Jamal dropped the rifle and covered his eyes with his hand. His shoulders shook. As the music surged, he stood, unsteady on his feet, and moved as if to embrace Tariq. But he fell to his knees, head down, arm extended, the other sleeve flapping uselessly. Half a Christ. Tariq removed his coat and shirt, took off his white T-shirt, and put shirt and coat back on. He lifted Jamal from the floor. St John Coltrane's saxophone wailed. He led him to the door, unlocked and opened it, and, white flag extended, ushered Jamal into the blinding glare outside.

Chapter 27

RACHEL saw the whole thing on television. After dropping Tariq home, she had returned to Crestwood, where she made herself a snack and sent him a text, asking him to call when he had the chance. At nine o'clock she tuned in to watch the news, and the siege at Jamal's house was live on every local channel. Tariq was inside by then and the cameras had fixed on the huddle of people behind the police van. His mother's blue hijab was a slash of brightness in the night, and the longer the standoff, the more it blazed.

She told him this late that night, when he called her after his parents had gone to bed.

'Got your text,' he said flatly. She laughed. They talked for an hour, a whisper at his end, her voice unrestrained. He was conscious the whole time that she was alone in her house.

He told her about the aftermath: Jamal whisked away, the chaos of liberation, Tariq's questioning by the police. When he had emerged from the station after midnight, his parents at his elbows, reporters trailed him to the car, the frozen breath of their shouted questions hanging in the night air like speech bubbles. His mother and father were in a daze. Malik had followed them to Jamal's house, arriving after Tariq had gone in. The scale of the crisis was overwhelming. On the way home, there was utter silence in the car. Every few minutes his mother reached back and touched his hand. At the house she prepared a small meal while

Malik asked tentative questions about the ordeal. The balance had shifted. After he left the kitchen, he heard his parents speaking Arabic in hushed tones.

He became a celebrity. His picture was in the papers and on the news; magazines and television shows wanted interviews. On the street strangers hailed him. Black people, especially, greeted him with clenched fists and wide smiles. Russell called him 'local hero' and gave him free food at the coffee shop. There was a peace service at the mosque, and the imam told his story. The school principal called his mother and said that the suspension had been rescinded; Tariq was welcome back without conditions, whenever he was ready.

But he did not feel like a hero. Though the world saw him as a lifesaver the episode in the house was unfinished business. He needed to see Jamal. The man was still in danger. All week, the police had refused to say where he was. He couldn't see him anyway, they told him, at least not until after Tariq's meeting with the crisis unit, his appointment with a psychiatrist and a 'critical incident stress debriefing'. There were protocols to observe, paperwork to be completed, decisions to be made. Policies and procedures. According to the press, Brad Jorgensen had declined to press charges, but the district attorney's office was preparing a criminal complaint. There would be a preliminary hearing, possibly a grand jury. Eventually Tariq learned that Jamal had been sent to a secure unit in the VA Hospital in Milwaukee, a hundred miles away. Visitors were not allowed, even if Tariq had been free to see him.

Rachel he could meet. Pestered when they met downtown, they escaped to Kayler Park, the Museum of Modern Art, a Middle Eastern music festival. They ice-skated on Verona Lake and drove to the Norse Lodge to watch the ski-jumping. She was ideal company. Everyone else in his life was on alert in his presence; Rachel absorbed all tension with a shake of her dark hair and a change of subject. She revived their catalogue of in-jokes and brought him small gifts: CDs, a tote bag, a Brahms bobblehead. They made fun of Christmas music and drank hot chocolate from a Thermos and fooled around when her parents were out. She took to calling him liquorice stick, a name she savoured.

Once the police routines had been completed, she urged him to go back to school. Only two weeks remained before the holiday break, but diving in now, she said, would get the bullshit over with and make the new year less distracting. So he returned, with her at his side to buffer the stares and comments. Beneath the winter-time aura of the classrooms, with their dry, cottony heat and odours of wet shoes and pencil shavings, Tariq sensed a deep change. His classmates seemed childish. The horse laughs and catchphrases of the boys, the girls' catty glances and straightened hair – it was as if he had been away for several years and returned as an observer. Classes grew tedious and claustrophobic. The lunchroom and hallways, once so terrifying, were rowdy and callow and awash with unwelcome attention. In this atmosphere of relentless posturing and cartoon behaviour, Rachel was an oasis.

At the end of the first week, Ms Wessell called him to her office. She was the same as ever, her pert face beaming good will, her wool blazer flecked with white and yellow, her awareness of her audience off kilter.

'You've had such an *eventful* month,' she said, hands fluttering, pen held high. 'How *are* you doing?'

'Fine.'

'Such an ordeal. And I understand you are seeing a police counsellor.'

'They're making me.'

'Well, it's a good idea, after what you've been through. You know, my office door is always open too.' He didn't answer. She tapped the desktop with her pen. 'I suppose you know that Brad Jorgensen has dropped out. I believe he's gone to work for his father.'

'I heard.'

'Of course, it's clear now why you were reluctant to tell us the whole story. It must have been very difficult.'

He nodded.

'Still,' she said, 'if there's anything...'

She shook her head, grinning maniacally. Behind her hung the mindless posters and school theme: EVERY STUDENT IS SPECIAL.

'One other thing,' she said at last, twiddling the pen. 'Mrs Gunderson was wondering if perhaps you'd like to address the civics class. Talk about, you know, the whole *situation* and how you handled it.'

He paused before replying. 'I don't think I'm ready for that, Ms Wessell.'

'Of course,' she said quickly, 'there's no rush. No pressure. It's so good you're back with us.'

As he left the counselling office, his English teacher, Ms Berman, walked by. She was not currently teaching; she'd had her baby and was on maternity leave.

'Tariq,' she said, eyebrows arched. 'The man of the moment.'

'Hello, Ms Berman.'

She wore skinny jeans and a lace top and had changed the colour of her hair from orange to ruby.

'Happy to be back?'

'I guess.'

'Get your head around *Hamlet* yet?'

'I think so.'

'How's Mr Butler?'

'OK. Not as good as you.'

She smiled and looked at the counsellor's office door. 'A word to the wise?' she said, dropping her voice. 'Don't let Wessell rope you in to any of her little schemes.'

Tariq shrugged. 'There are more things in heaven and earth than are dreamt of in her philosophy.'

She whooped in laughter and moved away. 'Keep reading, Tariq.'

HIS father flew to Mecca on the twenty-second of December. Zaida drove him to the airport through a dense snowfall, Tariq seated in the back. Dressed in *dishdasha*, round cap and sandals, Malik fretted in the passenger seat, worried that the weather would delay or cancel the flight. He had an hour in Chicago to make his connection to Frankfurt and then on to Riyadh. Even if every leg was on time, he would be travelling for twenty-five hours.

'I have to say *maghrib*,' he said. 'It's after sunset.'

'Don't worry,' Zaida said. 'We'll be there in time.'

Malik leaned forward and rubbed condensation from the windshield. From behind, his neck looked thin and frail. The swivelling beacons of ploughs and police vehicles flashed across the side of his face, reminding Tariq of the night of the siege. The car was cold, though the heater roared, eclipsing the murmur of his father's prayers.

Zaida drove carefully through the swirl of snowflakes. She wore a belted wool coat and leather gloves. And a fur hat. It was the first time in his life that Tariq had seen her outside the house without a hijab. And yet Malik had not seemed to notice.

Since the siege, his father had drawn further into himself. He did not engage with Tariq beyond the standard pleasantries.

He did not ask about school or Rachel or what was happening with the police. His mother told him that Malik was preparing to enter into *ihram*, a spiritual state of purity required of all pilgrims. He bathed at the mosque every day and wore a white tunic beneath his regular clothes. He was fastidious about daily prayers and recited the *talbiyah* over and over. He was not allowed to quarrel or commit acts of violence. Or have sex, Tariq knew from his reading, though his mother did not say that.

He did not exult in the reversal of their roles, but Tariq was relieved to be free of his father's attention. Though peace came at a price. Malik was like an old man. His religious fervour was a species of confusion. He was, literally, in another world. His mother, on the other hand, acted younger than ever. She was alert but relaxed, taking an interest in Tariq's progress at school, listening to him practise the clarinet, helping him complete the police forms. The previous Saturday, while Malik was at mosque, she had met Rachel and Tariq for lunch at Russell's coffee shop. She was not very comfortable with Rachel, but she did her best, talking to her about college plans and steering clear of delicate topics.

As soon as they had entered the airport terminal, Malik went to the men's room to perform ablutions. Tariq and his mother ordered tea at a café across the hall. As they sat and drank, they saw Malik emerge and spread his prayer mat on the floor, beside the shoeshine stand. They saw the people staring, making comments. The terminal was crowded with travellers coming and going for the holidays. The shops and check-in desks were decorated with lights and poinsettias, the high ceiling hung with red and green banners and pine garlands. Zaida sipped her tea reflectively, her hat on the chair beside her like a small animal.

After Malik had checked in, the family walked across the concourse to the security gates. Above them were arched steel buttresses and suspended walkways and enough space for an eagle to soar. Below, a floor so highly polished they could see their reflections. Shuffling in his sandals, clutching a leather-bound Qur'an, his father was like a figure from a different age. And yet he was also entirely familiar. Walking behind him, Tariq could see the world as he did, a view that saw no contradiction between ancient prayers and twenty-first-century systems. There was nothing that could not be synthesised. And yet the two of them had found so little common ground. Mecca, finally, was home for Malik. Not Monroe.

At the entry to the security line, Tariq looked away while his parents said their goodbyes. Then his father embraced him.

'Tariq,' he whispered, 'forgive me.' They clutched each other. 'And look after your mother. She is on your watch now.'

He smelled of incense and hair oil. As they disengaged, Malik dropped his chin and dabbed his eyes. Then he was walking away, shoulders hunched, his pants sagging in the seat, his sandals slapping the floor.

'Malik!' Zaida cried.

He turned and waved and disappeared into the crowd.

Tariq grew aware of the terminal's noise and tumult. The piped music and thunderous echo. Released from the purpose of being there, he and his mother were suddenly keen to leave. He followed her out into the cold.

Briskly they made their way to the parking lot. Night had fallen and the skies had cleared. The stars were dense and milky. To the south the lights of the city glowed dully. A dusting of snow covered the car and, while his mother started the engine, Tariq cleared the windows.

He climbed in and strapped on his seatbelt. His mother waited for the heater to clear the windshield's condensation.

'Tariq?' she said.

Her tone was odd. She was motionless, hands folded in her lap.

'Yes, Ommi,' he said.

'I'll miss him, you know.'

'I know.'

Slowly she pulled on her gloves, as if waiting for more from him. When he didn't say anything else, she said, 'Would you like to go out for dinner?'

Chapter 28

THE STATION PLATFORM was dark and dirty, its soiled canopy fringed with Christmas lights, the waiting buses spattered with mud and salt. It was solidly cold, close to zero, with a slicing wind from the north. But Tariq felt good. It was a new year. His wounds had healed. The blackened snow and trash-lined fences didn't bother him. The stinging frost went unnoticed. He had a clear head and the fresh view of a pilgrim.

The trip to Milwaukee would take almost three hours, with stops in several towns along the way. His fellow passengers – soldiers on leave, harried young mothers, unshaven men with battered bags – called to mind Jamal's stories of drifting across America. Tariq's seat was lumpy, but the window was clean and the bus well-heated. He settled in with new headphones for his iPod and a jumbo box of Junior Mints. Stowed above him on the luggage rack were his clarinet case, several music magazines and a carton of stuffed pastries his mother had baked the night before.

The VA Hospital had called and told him he could visit. Conditions were strict: he could come only between two and four in the afternoon, a policeman would be present, he would be searched on the way in for contraband. At the preliminary hearing, the judge had found probable cause and bound Jamal over for trial. He was formally under arrest. But he was being represented by Rachel's father and, though Jamal had waived his right to a jury trial, Mr Katz was confident that a diagnosis of post-traumatic stress disorder would lead to charges being dropped.

The bus left Monroe on time. Within ten minutes it was out of city grime and moving past frozen fields, grain silos, covered bridges. The airbase shimmered in the distance, jets parked on the runway in a haze of frost. Beyond the dipping telephone wires were groves of bare trees, lone birds flashing in the wind, small lakes dotted with ice-fishing huts. Snow stretched as far as the horizon, as pure and undulating as desert sand.

Tariq ate mints by the handful and watched the landscape skim past to a soundtrack of Iraqi folk music. The frost hung like powder beneath a dim sun. A dog ran from a farmyard, barking soundlessly. As they neared Lake Ripley his phone chimed. A text message: *o mother the handsome man tortures me ... have a gd trip and gd luck with j. love rachel*

He fell asleep and woke in Fort Atkinson, disoriented. The hydraulic hiss of closing doors brought a flash of memory: climbing onto a bus in Baghdad at four in the morning, clutching his mother's hand. No gunfire, for once, though soldiers with AK-47s prowled the streets. Children like himself cried in the darkness. Smells of diesel exhaust and dew-soaked vegetation. His father clutching paperwork and speaking furtively with the bus driver. The bus pulling away. Rahim trotting alongside, waving from the shadows. His parents weeping.

Since returning from Mecca, his father had melted into the edges of Tariq's life. He wore only traditional clothes and prayed constantly. When he wasn't at work he was at mosque or in his room. His religion was no longer a lash but a personal consolation. The house was at peace. Zaida had spent the holiday break grading papers and planning courses for the new semester. As if to balance Malik's ascetic fervour, she wore bright skirts and stylish tops and a pair of calf boots she had bought at the New Year sales. His father had become stricter in his interpretation of what was *halal*, so she did all her food shopping at the International Market or the Masjid Co-op. Meals were better than ever.

The bus descended through Milwaukee's frozen suburbs. From Union Station Tariq walked to the hospital, past Mitchell Park and funereal government buildings and the deserted baseball stadium. The wind was bitter, the city shackled in ice. Steam billowed from manhole covers and homeless men, layered in old coats and knitted hats, gathered above ventilation grilles. By the time he got to the VA he was stiff with the cold. The entrance canopy glittered in the sun, which lit up the huge American flag hanging on the building face.

Jamal was in a private room on the fourth floor. It had been decorated like an ordinary bedroom, but the windows were barred and an antiseptic smell soaked the air. The heat was cranked up high. Dressed in hospital pyjamas, he was playing cribbage with his police guard, a young black man with perfect teeth and almond eyes and a uniform so new the shirt still bore creases from its packaging.

'Whoa, liquorice stick man! Come over here.'

They hugged. Jamal was shaky. His breath was bad. His shaved head shone under the fluorescent lights. From his bare neck hung a leather medallion of a map of Africa striped in Rasta colours.

'You cold?' Jamal asked.

'Freezing.'

'Say hello to Marcus, the young man who be *guarding* my ass.'

'Hey now, Mr Pierce. It's my detail.'

Tariq shook the policeman's hand. Shy and bright-eyed, he carried himself like an athlete, at ease in his body and with smooth skin that seemed to shine from within. He wasn't much older than Tariq.

'Take a guess where my man here is from,' Jamal said.

'I have no idea.'

'High Point, North Carolina.'

Marcus said, 'Greensboro, actually.'

'Shit, close enough. Tell him, Tariq.'

'Where John Coltrane grew up.'

'What I say? Course, up to two days ago he no idea who Trane *is*.'

'Mr Pierce is educating me about music.'

'About *life*, son.'

Jamal's voice was out of tune. Beside Marcus's natural ease he was like a dog in a kennel: smile tight, muscles tensed, teeth bared.

Tariq took the carton of pastries from his bag and set it beside the cribbage board. 'My mother sent these.'

Jamal's head twitched like a bird's. 'Bless her soul. Marcus, what say you get us some coffee?'

Marcus nodded slowly, the corners of his mouth tugged downwards. 'I can do that.'

With Marcus gone, Jamal grew quiet. The room was spare. The bed was mussed but clean. Beside it, on a rollaway table, was a stack of paperbacks and a copy of the *Journal Sentinel*. A scatter of cards and letters. Jamal had plastic bracelets on both wrists. His cloudy eyes avoided Tariq's.

He tasted a pastry and shook his head. 'That's a long bus ride.'

'Not too bad.'

The top paperback was by John Grisham. 'Are you reading that?' Tariq asked.

'Marcus, he brings in the books. The card games. But I can't concentrate.'

'What about the letters?'

Jamal smiled wanly. 'Oh, I'm a project. People saw me on TV, want to show me the light.'

The letters were from churches, charitable institutions, societies, lonely women, crackpots. People, Jamal said, in the rescue business.

People who had no clue. Who thought words could solve every human problem.

'What about the hospital here? Do they have you on a programme?'

'Is Zoloft a programme? I do group therapy and some one-on-one shit. The way they tell it, it's all good.'

'But you don't think so?'

Jamal snorted.

'And Mr Katz, he's looking after the case, right?'

'I suppose,' Jamal said.

'Well *that's* good, isn't it?'

The radiators creaked. Jamal's mouth had tightened to a hard slot. His chin was puckered and a milky film rose in his eyes. He breathed deeply, and as his chest expanded Tariq could sense the fear fluttering inside.

'Not the case I'm worried about,' Jamal said. 'It's the evil in my head.'

'Don't say that.'

He pointed towards the hallway. 'You seen what's out there. The cripples. The loonies. Oh yeah, I *found* my scene. Marcus, he got the easiest job in Milwaukee. He *knows* I ain't moving. I don't need no guard. I hear those wheelchairs in the halls and I want to split my head against the wall. Bars on the window, but they ain't jail bars. We're on the fourth floor. They know what I'm capable of.'

'Only you know that, Jamal. Only you can change it.'

Jamal's temple twitched, blood and tendon jumping to the tug of fear within. It brought Tariq back to the last moments in the house, surrounded by guns. Klieg-light scrutiny and SWAT muscle just beyond the door. What could be worse than that?

Sitting on the bed, Jamal plucked at folds in the sheet. 'Oh yeah. It's that simple.'

'That's not what I meant.'

Jamal looked up, eyes keen, mouth open, gold tooth like a coin in the snow. 'You know who was here yesterday?'

'Who?'

'Naima.'

'Your daughter.'

He nodded, eyes popping, then suddenly dropped his head, overcome. An ashy shadow fell across his noble features. His brow was stippled with sweat.

'Charmaine brought her. Credit the bitch. Though she stayed downstairs. Sent the child up with a nurse.'

'Is she going to be in the parade again this year? Maybe you can go and see her.'

'If I'm not in prison.'

'You won't be.'

The windows, filigreed with ice, had darkened in the winter afternoon. In spite of its soft chairs and patterned wallpaper, the room had a pale-green institutional chill. The floor had several brown scars, where the linoleum had split.

'You know what she said? "I saw you on television, Daddy." That's how my baby found out.'

'And she came to see you.'

Jamal sighed, a deep, trembling exhalation. Beneath the harsh lights his face had a bluish tint and his eyes were as yellow as a dog's. Tariq felt the creep of a familiar despair. Where feeling grew tangled and dark and words lost all meaning. From the hallway came hospital sounds. Doctors being paged. Nurses laughing. The squeak of trollies on the polished floor.

They were silent for a while. Then Tariq remembered the clarinet case. He walked across the split linoleum and closed the door. Took his instrument from the case and assembled it. As he warmed up,

Jamal sat up in the bed and crossed his legs. The clarinet's thin, bleating tone spiralled in the overheated room.

He played 'In a Sentimental Mood'. The melody, which had been so difficult when he first tried it, came effortlessly. He'd been practising. The secret to jazz, he had discovered, was the same as *choubi*. Master the tune so that you no longer had to think about it. Concentrate on the rhythm. The notes, free to breathe, to waver, to reach, took on an existence of their own. They filled the room like the wind, invisible but powerful, finding a way through barriers of blood and skin to the soul, what the imam called *rouhi*.

The reed buzzed against his lip. He closed his eyes and let the song soar, bending notes, adding trills and grace notes and throwing in a little Iraqi funk. He heard Jamal shout *yeah*. The old Jamal, hip and intense. Marcus arrived carrying a cardboard tray of coffee cups. He sat in the chair beside the door and listened, grinning, tapping his foot.

In the vault of feeling created by the music, Tariq let his mind gather images of those who were important to him: Rachel dancing, slowly, sinuously, her body moving to the line of melody like a scarf in the hand of a magician; Rahim in the mortuary, his bloodless face peaceful and composed; his father, walking counter-clockwise around the Kaaba, kissing the Black Stone; and his mother in her new clothes, arranging the pictures and mementoes on her desk and ushering students into her office. All the world was there for him to float above, buoyed by the music. The mosque, the high school, the parking lot. And in the middle of it all, Jamal, as he had been and would be again: tall and elegant, like an African chief, jaw set, head high, teeth flashing. His earring sparkling like phosphorous. Listening to the aching notes of an old jazz tune, as pure as love.

A Love Supreme

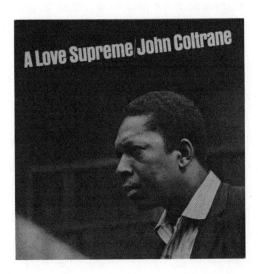

ON a cold December afternoon in 1964, in the church-like Van Gelder Recording Studio in northern New Jersey, the jazz saxophonist John Coltrane and his quartet recorded *A Love Supreme*, a work of enduring musical and religious significance that, over fifty years later, continues to have a profound impact.

'During the year 1957, I experienced, by the grace of God, a spiritual awakening which was to lead me to a richer, fuller, more productive life,' Coltrane wrote in the album's original liner notes. 'At the time, I humbly asked to be given the means and privilege to make others happy through music. This album is a humble offering to Him.'

Millions of people have bought *A Love Supreme*, making it one of the most successful jazz recordings of all time. The manuscript for the album is in the National Museum of American History in Washington, DC, and the saxophone that Coltrane used to record the piece was recently given to the Smithsonian Museum. Enthralled by its magnificent outpouring of sound and its paradoxical genius – simple yet complex, violent yet peaceful – listeners have responded not just to its musical greatness but also to its intense, restless search for spiritual meaning.

Coltrane's 'spiritual awakening' helped him overcome drug and alcohol problems and led him over time to produce this great devotional work. He was supported throughout this period of quest by his wife Naima, who was a convert to Islam. Though intensely private about the roots of his conversion, Coltrane used phrases and rhythms from the Qur'an in the piece itself, and in the poem that he wrote to accompany 'Psalm', the work's final movement. The album is a key document in the link between jazz and Islam, an important connection that is part of the greater African-American history of seeking dignity, difference and transcendence in the Muslim faith.

A Love Supreme is, thus, part of two great traditions that intersect in mid-twentieth-century America, musical and religious. It is one of the great pieces of music of the twentieth century, and a fully realised spiritual work, all the more remarkable for its appearance in one of the least spiritual of times. As Coltrane said after recording it, 'I'd like to point out to people the divine in a musical language that transcends words. I want to speak to their souls.'

About the publisher

LITTLE ISLAND is an award-winning Dublin-based publisher and has been producing books for young people since 2010. We are five years old this year and have just published our fiftieth book, but this is our first adult title.

For more about Little Island and to buy our books online visit us at:

www.littleisland.ie

Little Island